10/18 DATE DUE

JUN 09 2020	
APR 01 2023	

BL: 5.2 AR: 7Pts Q# 197618

GRENADE

Also by Alan Gratz

Refugee
Projekt 1065
Prisoner B-3087
Code of Honor
Ban This Book
The Brooklyn Nine
Samurai Shortstop

ALAN GRATZ

GRENADE

Scholastic Press / New York

Library of Congress Cataloging-in-Publication Data available

ISBN 978-1-338-24569-1

10 9 8 7 6 5 4 3 2 1 18 19 20 21 22

Printed in the U.S.A. 23
First edition, October 2018
Book design by Nina Goffi

For Niki Winters

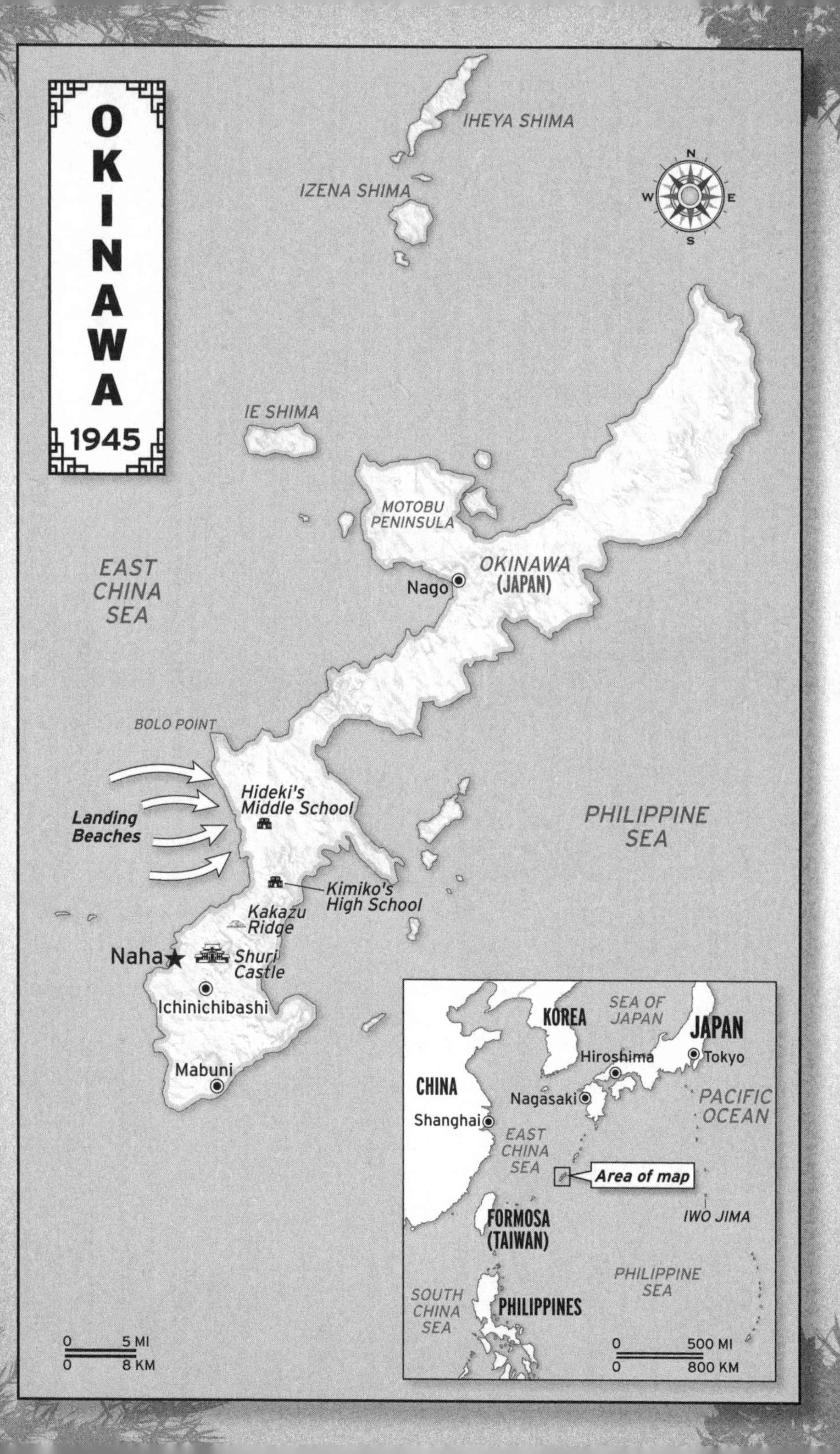
OKINAWA
1945
IHEYA SHIMA
IZENA SHIMA
N
W
E
S
IE SHIMA
MOTOBU
PENINSULA
OKINAWA
(JAPAN)
Nago
EAST
CHINA
SEA
BOLO POINT
Hideki's
Middle School
Landing
Beaches
PHILIPPINE
SEA
Kimiko's
High School
Kakazu
Ridge
Naha
Shuri
Castle
Ichinichibashi
Mabuni
0 5 MI
0 8 KM
KOREA
SEA OF
JAPAN
JAPAN
Hiroshima
Tokyo
CHINA
Nagasaki
PACIFIC
OCEAN
Shanghai
EAST
CHINA
SEA
Area of map
FORMOSA
(TAIWAN)
IWO JIMA
PHILIPPINE
SEA
SOUTH
CHINA
SEA
PHILIPPINES
0 500 MI
0 800 KM

A NOTE TO THE READER:

This book contains terminology that
was used during World War II
in order to accurately reflect
the historical time period.

PART ONE

HIDEKI

THE END

APRIL 1, 1945

An American bomb landed a hundred meters away— *Kra-KOOM!*—and the school building exploded. Hideki Kaneshiro ducked and screamed with all the other boys as they were showered with rocks and splinters.

Hideki couldn't believe it—one minute his school was there, the next it was gone. Worse, the bombs meant that the American battleships had found them! He turned to run.

"Don't move! Nobody is to move!"

Hideki froze. Every atom of his being told him to *RUN*. To find a cave somewhere to hide. But Lieutenant Colonel Sano's voice was so commanding, so forceful, that he didn't move. No one did. Even the governor of Okinawa, who was already three steps toward a shelter, stopped in his tracks.

"Return to your ranks!" Lieutenant Colonel Sano yelled.

Hideki inched back into line with the other boys and stood at attention, his heart pounding. Takeshi, another fourth-year boy, whimpered softly beside him. Katsumasa, who was Takeshi's best friend, stood ramrod straight, a bead of sweat rolling down his face.

"What's the matter, babies?" Yoshio whispered from the row of students behind them. "Ready to run home to Mommy?"

Hideki's neck burned hot with shame for being scared. Yoshio was a fifth-year boy who had made it his personal mission to terrorize all the fourth-year boys—especially Hideki. Yoshio was half a head taller than Hideki, with arms as big as tree trunks and a face full of chicken pox scars that made him look twice as old. Hideki had always been the smallest boy in the school, and Yoshio had never let him forget it. Hideki was fourteen years old but looked like he was twelve, with a round boyish face, thin arms and legs, and short-cropped black hair.

Hideki had to keep an ear open for whatever stunt Yoshio might pull behind him. But the rest of him was transfixed on what was happening in front of him. If he could have moved without being scolded, Hideki would have made a rectangle with his fingers like a photographer had shown him once, to frame a picture of what he was seeing. And what a picture it would have made.

A hundred boys stood in a small clearing outside what was left of their middle school. All of them wore their tan Imperial Japanese Army uniforms and caps. It was almost two o'clock in the morning, and it was dark. The ground shook with the heavy booms of artillery shells falling all around them, fired by American battleships offshore. A single flickering lamp cast an eerie, dreamlike glimmer on two rows of students standing on one side of the schoolyard, and a row of teachers on the other.

In the middle stood their principal, Norio Kojima, alongside the governor of Okinawa and Lieutenant Colonel Sano of the Imperial Japanese Army.

Hideki studied Sano, who stood rigid in his khaki uniform and knee-high leather boots. A sword hung from the lieutenant colonel's belt, and the breast of his jacket was crowded with colorful ribbons. Hideki knew that all the other boys were as spellbound by Sano as he was. Sano was the one they wanted to be.

They were gathered here now, outside their bomb shelters, because tonight Hideki and his classmates were graduating early. The governor of Okinawa and a Japanese lieutenant colonel usually weren't in attendance at graduation, and the ceremony wasn't usually held at two o'clock in the morning. But then, it wasn't every day America invaded your island either.

Today was the end of everything Hideki had ever known.

"Later this morning, the enemy will land on Okinawa," Lieutenant Colonel Sano announced in his imposing voice as the bombs continued to fall. "American devils, whose only purpose is to kill you and your families in the most brutal, merciless ways possible."

Hideki shuddered, hoping that Sano—and Yoshio—wouldn't notice.

"They will hunt your grandparents down and burn them alive," Sano continued. "They will torture your mothers. Butcher your brothers and sisters. They will try to trick you too. Offer you food and kindness. But the food they carry is poisoned, and the hand that beckons you with friendship hides the one behind their back, holding a grenade."

Kra-KOOM!

Another bomb exploded nearby, destroying a tree that had stood for generations, but no one was going anywhere now. Sano had their attention.

Hideki knew that America and Japan had been at war for almost four years, fighting each other all over the Pacific in places like the Solomon Islands, the Philippines, and Iwo Jima. Then, a year ago, the Imperial Japanese

Army had arrived in force on Okinawa to dig defenses for the inevitable American invasion.

Okinawa was a tiny island, just a hundred and ten kilometers long and eleven kilometers wide. It lay south of the Japanese mainland and had once been an independent kingdom, with its own language and religion. But Japan had annexed Okinawa and made it a province back when Hideki's grandparents were children. And now, because Okinawa belonged to Japan, the American army was coming to attack.

"From this moment," Sano went on, his voice heavy with importance, "you have graduated from students to soldiers. You are now the Blood and Iron Student Corps. Each of you must be ready to die a glorious death in the name of the Emperor. This is your island. It is *you* who should be fighting for it, not the Imperial Japanese Army! You must fight like demons to protect your homeland. One plane for one battleship, one man for ten of the enemy!"

Another bomb exploded nearby, and Hideki cowered. He agreed with Sano, but if this ceremony went on too much longer he would never get to trade his life for ten American soldiers. An American battleship would kill him and all the rest of the students with one shot.

Fearless as he was, Sano seemed to come to the same conclusion. He nodded, and one of his lieutenants went down the row and put two grenades into the hands of each middle schooler.

Hideki glanced at Takeshi and Katsumasa in disbelief—the IJA was giving them real grenades!

Hideki accepted his two grenades. Each was cylindrical, like a drinking cup, and weighed about a pound. They were a little bigger than Hideki's hands and looked like pineapple-shaped lanterns painted shiny black.

"What's this?" Yoshio asked, and Hideki turned to look. Yoshio had been given two grenades that were very different from Hideki's. Yoshio's grenades were made out of pottery!

"The American naval blockade has made metal scarce," the lieutenant explained. "Some of you will be given ceramic grenades."

"Ceramic?" Yoshio said when the lieutenant moved down the line. "But if these crack, they're useless!" He glanced up, saw Hideki had been given two metal grenades, and quickly took them without asking, pushing his pottery grenades into Hideki's hands with a wolfish grin. Hideki wanted to complain, but he knew it was pointless—and would only make things worse with Yoshio.

Hideki examined the glazed brown pottery grenades he'd been stuck with. They were the size and shape of baseballs, and much lighter than the real metal grenades.

Inside the small rubber cap at the top, there was a match-like fuse and a little piece of rough wood. You activated the grenade by striking the fuse against the wood, but Hideki had no idea how fast the fuse burned and how long he would have before the grenade exploded.

The complicated trigger distressed him, and the soft *clink* of the delicate pottery grenades against each other made him worried that they *would* crack—or worse, explode in his jacket pocket.

But if these grenades work, Hideki thought, *I can finally overcome my family's curse. I can prove to Lieutenant Colonel Sano and to Yoshio and to everyone that I really* am *brave. And I can make the Kaneshiro family fearless again.*

"One grenade is for the American monsters coming to kill your family," Sano told them, and Hideki looked up. Sano's gaze swept down the row of boys until it stopped on Hideki, like he was talking to him alone. "Then, after you have killed as many Americans as you can," Sano added, "you are to use the other grenade to kill yourself."

RAY

OPERATION ICEBERG

APRIL 1, 1945

Private Ray Majors took a nervous peek over the side of the boat carrying him and his squad across the choppy waves toward Okinawa. Through the salty sea spray, he saw every American ship in the bay—more than a thousand of them—shooting their guns at the island. Battleships, destroyers, cruisers. And overhead, wave after wave of planes flew over the island, dropping agony and death from above. All to protect the sitting-duck GIs and Marines like Ray in their little boats.

One of the battleships' big guns was so loud and so close that the *BOOM* rattled Ray's stomach. This was it. The real deal. The invasion of Okinawa. What the brass called "Operation Iceberg," even though an iceberg wouldn't have survived ten seconds in this blazing heat. It was Ray's first battle of the war, and it was a big one.

It was all Ray could do not to pee his green pants. But he was almost relieved to finally be going into battle. For weeks, he and two hundred other Marines had been holed up with twenty Sherman tanks in the dark belly of a rolling, creaking ship as Japanese suicide bombers came dropping out of the sky at them. As far as Ray was concerned, being trapped like a rat in the bottom of a ship was ten times worse than being on deck and watching the kamikazes come in.

But then, at last, had come H-Hour: 8:30 a.m., April 1st. Easter Sunday, 1945. Code name: "Love Day." The day that Ray and the other 183,000 American soldiers and Marines of the Tenth Army finally boarded amphibious troop carriers and headed east toward the beaches of Okinawa.

The fact that Love Day was also April Fool's Day had not been lost on a single one of them.

When he'd enlisted in the Marines a few months ago, Ray had never thought he'd end up on a boat four hundred miles from Japan. He thought he'd be sent to Europe, to fight Hitler and the Nazis. But Allied forces had just freed France and crossed the Rhine River into Germany, and the end of the war in Europe was near. Everybody could sense it.

But the war against Japan was far from over. Almost four years ago, the Japanese had sneak-attacked Pearl Harbor, a US naval base in the Hawaiian Islands. Ray remembered exactly where he was when he'd heard the news—sitting in a soda shop with Tibby Lundgren, her blond hair shining in the bright afternoon sun. Their first date. His first ever date with *anybody*. The music on the radio had come to a sudden stop, and a reporter had read the shocking news. Battleships sunk. Airplanes burning on the runway. Almost twenty-five hundred Americans dead and a thousand more wounded. Ray understood then that life as he knew it—the farm, high school, Tibby Lundgren—all of it was over.

A day later, President Roosevelt declared war against Japan, and Ray ran away from home to join the Marines. They wouldn't take him though—they made him wait until he was eighteen.

Ray shifted uncomfortably on the metal bench, remembering the belt-whipping his father had given him when he'd slunk back home.

The acrid, sickly sweet smell of someone vomiting in the boat brought Ray back to the here and now. The rocking of the boat made Ray feel sick too, and he went through the equipment in his pack to distract himself. Flashlight, pistol, canteen, first aid kit, extra cartridges for his M-1 rifle. The Marine-issue "entrenching tool," which as far as Ray could tell was just a shovel with a fancy name.

And then there were the grenades. Two of them. Cast iron. Each one was about the size of a pear, but round in the middle and tapered at the top and bottom. The raised squares on them made them look like pineapples. Each was painted a drab olive green, the army's favorite color, and had a bright yellow collar around the neck. To activate the grenade, you gripped the gray handle on the side and pulled a big wire ring attached to a pin. The grenade activated when you let go of the handle, igniting the fuse. Then you had just four or five seconds before it went boom.

In another pocket, Ray found the brochure Naval Command had given him and all the other Marines to explain the difference between Okinawans and Japanese. Apparently, there *was* a difference. The brochure said the Okinawans were generally smaller, and were "simple, polite, law-abiding, and peaceful." If they could help it, the Marines were supposed to pass Okinawan civilians on to the shelters being set up for their relief by the military government. But the brochure also warned that the Marines might get a chilly reception from Okinawans: *All they know about Americans they get from Tokyo propaganda*, it said. *So you can expect them to look at you as though you were a cross between Dracula and Frankenstein's monster—at first, anyway.*

The handout included some Japanese phrases to help draw the Okinawans from hiding, and Ray had been practicing them in the dark hold of the ship for the past two weeks.

"DEY-tey ko-ee," he sounded out now. *Come out.* "hee-DOY koat-o wa shee ma-SEN." *You will not be hurt.*

"Forget all that stuff," said Corporal John Barboza, who sat across from Ray. Big John—as everyone called him—was an enormous guy from the Bronx, New York, who'd probably been shaving since he was five.

Ray, with his close-cropped sandy brown hair, short legs, and round freckled face, looked young enough to be Big John's son—even though Big John couldn't have been more than five years older than him.

Big John was one of the few members of the 1st Marines to survive the division's last battle in the Philippines. He was also Ray's designated foxhole buddy.

"A Jap's a Jap, Majors," Big John told him. "You want my advice? Shoot them before they shoot you. That's how you survive."

"Your last name is Majors?" asked their squad leader, Sergeant Walter Meredith. The sergeant was tall and lean and tan and had been with the 1st Marines even longer than Big John had. "This kid needs a nickname, pronto. The enemy hears us calling him 'Majors,' they'll think we're talking to a real Marine major and throw everything they've got at him."

Ray felt the blood drain from his face. How was that fair? He hadn't picked his last name!

"Where ya from, kid?" another Marine asked.

"Norfolk, Nebraska," Ray replied.

"'Cornhusker,' then."

"No, 'Babyface'! Kid looks like he's thirteen."

"'Shorty,'" somebody else suggested.

"Let's wait and see if the kid survives the beach landing," Big John said. "Then we can worry about a nickname for him."

That shut everybody up, and they starting thinking again about what was coming when they hit the beaches.

"They say it'll be even worse than Peleliu, and we got the holy crap kicked out of us there."

"I hear the Japs are waiting for us behind a ten-foot concrete wall with machine guns every six feet."

"I bet eighty percent of us don't make it off the beaches."

Ray's arms and legs felt weak. Shaky, like at the end of a day working hard on the farm when he'd skipped lunch.

Sergeant Meredith patted him on the knee. "Don't worry, kid. Just keep your head down and move as fast as you can."

Ray nodded anxiously, and his oversized helmet slid down over his eyes.

The boat's motor shifted down, and they could all hear it and feel it. They were slowing to run up on the beach.

No—I'm not ready, Ray thought. *I'm not ready. I'm not—*

"All right, Marines!" Sergeant Meredith yelled. "This is it! Stay low, don't bunch up, and run like hell!"

The boat lurched to a stop, and suddenly the ramp at the front dropped into the water with a splash.

Ray grabbed his rifle and ran like hell.

HIDEKI

THE DIVINE WIND

Hideki had never seen so many ships in his entire life.

He and other boys of the Blood and Iron Student Corps stood on a hillside overlooking the ocean. Below them were hundreds—maybe thousands—of American ships. Huge ones too, bigger than any Japanese ship Hideki had ever seen in Naha Harbor.

Hideki made a rectangle shape with his fingers and peered through it.

When the Imperial Japanese Army had arrived on Okinawa, they'd brought a photographer with them: Lieutenant Tanaka. His job was to take pictures of Okinawa so the generals could formulate their defense. Lieutenant Tanaka had told the school that he needed someone local, an Okinawan, to show him around the area and carry his camera equipment for him. Hideki had been given the job.

Lieutenant Tanaka had lots of different cameras—some that used rolls of film and could be carried on a strap around the neck, others that clicked and whirred and took moving pictures. But the photographer's favorite was a beast of a camera that stretched out like an accordion and stood on a tripod. Because it was so big and heavy and took so long to set up, Lieutenant Tanaka would frame his shots through his fingers first. He showed Hideki how to do it too.

"What story does the picture tell?" Lieutenant Tanaka had said to Hideki. "That's what I'm always asking myself. Not just what's happening in the photograph I take, but what happened before it was taken, and what will happen afterward. How you frame a photo says everything about the story you're trying to tell."

Hideki framed a shot of the battleships at sea through his fingers. The story it told wasn't a good one for Okinawa. "We'll never hold out against all those ships," he whispered to himself.

"What's the matter, Hideki? Chicken?"

Hideki hadn't thought anyone could hear him, but of course Yoshio had. He punched Hideki in the shoulder, hard, making him flinch.

"Hideki thinks we're going to lose!" Yoshio announced, and all the other boys laughed.

"No," Hideki protested, his face hot. "I just—"

"The *Yamato* will be here soon, and it'll smash those American ships!" Yoshio said. The *Yamato* was the biggest battleship ever constructed, and the pride of the Imperial Japanese Navy. If the *Yamato* did come, the Americans would have a real battle on their hands. But wherever the *Yamato* was, it wasn't here.

"Hey. I just realized," Yoshio said. "Hideki's never been through the Gauntlet of Fists!"

Hideki blanched. *No*. Not here. Not now! The Gauntlet of Fists was a tradition at his middle school—a brutal tradition. The fifth-years would line up in two rows and send one fourth-year running down the lane between them, punching him with their fists as he went. Fourth-years who made it through the Gauntlet came out bruised and bleeding. Those who didn't were sent to the nurse's station with broken arms and legs. Hideki thought that he had escaped his trip through the Gauntlet, but Yoshio had other ideas. He grabbed Hideki by the arm and told the other fifth-years to line up.

"You—you can't!" Hideki cried. "We're not in school anymore. There aren't any more fifth-years and fourth-years. We're all members of the Blood and Iron Student Corps."

"What does that matter?" Yoshio said. "We're still bigger and older than you."

Hideki closed his eyes and braced for the first punch.

"Look!" another fourth-year cried. "Kamikazes!"

Hideki opened his eyes and looked up. A squadron of Japanese planes had emerged from the clouds. Yoshio let go of Hideki, and together all the boys ran to the edge of the cliff to watch. The Japanese kamikazes waited until they were right on top of the American fleet and then dive-bombed straight for the battleships.

"Kamikaze" meant "Divine Wind" in Japanese. Hideki remembered learning about it in school. Hundreds of years ago, the Chinese emperor Kublai Khan sent a huge armada of ships to attack the Japanese mainland. There was no way the Japanese could have defeated them, and it looked like China would conquer Japan forever. But then a vicious typhoon had risen up in the Sea of Japan. The storm wrecked most of the ships and scattered the rest, and Kublai Khan was defeated. The Japanese believed their emperor was divine, and that heaven had saved them. They called the typhoon the Kamikaze, the Divine Wind, and they believed even now that Japan could never be conquered—even if they were losing, at the last minute a Divine Wind would come along and save them.

Just like these kamikazes had saved Hideki here and now.

Not quite willing to wait on the heavens to save

them, the Imperial Japanese Army had organized a last-ditch Divine Wind of their own. Today's kamikazes were special attack planes that flew missions from Japanese air bases, never intending to return. They were loaded down with as many bombs and explosives as they could carry, and a kamikaze pilot's only mission was to crash his plane into an Allied ship in a suicide attack.

Hideki's heart swelled at the sight of the planes dropping out of the sky into the withering antiaircraft fire of the giant American ships. *This* was true bravery, he thought. To fight in the face of overwhelming odds. Not like him, cowering and hiding from Yoshio, hoping for a battle to spare him from a beating.

Hideki thought about his cowardly ancestor, Shigetomo. Centuries ago, Shigetomo had surrendered without a fight when Japanese samurai had invaded Okinawa. His family had been spared, but the samurai cut off Shigetomo's head even though he hadn't fought back.

On Okinawa, you lived under the same roof with the spirits of your ancestors. The shadow of that decision—the 350-year-old ghost of their cowardly forefather—had haunted Hideki's family for hundreds of years. It haunted Hideki still.

One of the kamikazes twisted through the hail of tracer fire and dove straight into the tail of an American destroyer. It hit with a fierce explosion that boomed across the water, and fire and black smoke poured from the deck of the ship.

"*Banzai!*" Hideki yelled with the other boys, and they danced and pumped their fists in the air.

But then Hideki quieted. Deep down, he knew the truth: The kamikaze plane that had hit the destroyer was the only one that had gotten through. Dozens more kamikaze planes were being shot down by American ships long before they ever got close to the armada. Again and again the kamikazes exploded into bright red balls of flame, and the pieces of their planes tumbled harmlessly to the sea. This was a battle the Divine Wind was not going to win.

Soon, the other boys quieted down as well. When the fifth-years tired of watching the kamikazes, Hideki knew they would turn on him again. *Yoshio* would turn on him again. Send him through the Gauntlet of Fists. He was sure of it. Unless Hideki could think of something else to distract them.

Hideki couldn't see the beach where the American transports were landing, but it had to be close. He pulled one of the grenades from his jacket pocket and hefted it with bravado.

"The army probably has something special planned for the American monsters when they hit the beaches,"

Hideki cried, "but let's go kill the ones who get through!"

Hideki's classmates cheered again, and he sighed with relief as they ran off ahead of him into the forest. Anything was better than facing the Gauntlet of Fists—even American guns.

RAY

LOVE DAY

Blood pounded in Ray's ears as he staggered into the waist-high surf, his heart beating a thousand times a second. His helmet slid down over his eyes again, and he struggled to push it up. He plunged headlong through the waves and tried to keep his rifle out of the water. The pack on his back felt like it weighed ten tons and was going to drag him down with it.

Stay low, don't bunch up, and run like hell, he repeated to himself. He high-stepped the waves when he could, separating himself from the other Marines so they wouldn't make such easy targets. He crouched low, his whole body clenched in anticipation of the machine gun fire—

—which never came. Only after he'd scrambled over the broken remains of a seawall and lurched up onto the beach did Ray realize there was nobody to shoot—and nobody shooting at him. Besides the giant craters left by the navy's artillery, it was just a white, sandy beach with low, rolling green hills beyond. No ten-foot sea-wall, no mines, no barbed wire, no machine gun nests. Nothing.

There's got to be some mistake, thought Ray. Where were all the bodies? The wrecked vehicles? The machine guns and mortars everyone had promised would blow him apart?

One of the Sherman tanks fitted out with pontoons to help it through the surf clanked to a stop nearby. The tank commander popped up from the top hatch to see it with his own two eyes. He tipped his helmet back and scratched his head, clearly as perplexed as Ray and everyone else. Out at sea, Japanese kamikazes were buzzing the American and British battleships like flies, but here on the island the Japanese army wasn't putting up any resistance at all.

The rest of Ray's company splashed up around him.

"Where are the Japs?" someone asked.

"Looks like they've taken a powder!" said one of the new guys.

"Man, this is almost scarier than being shot at," Big John said. He propped his big Browning Automatic Rifle on his shoulder. The Browning, what the others called a "BAR," was so heavy it came with its own bipod to rest the barrel on, but Big John was so strong he carried it the way Ray carried his much lighter rifle.

"Did the navy barrage kill them all?" Ray asked.

Big John shook his head. "That seawall we walked over, yeah. But there weren't nobody defending it, or there'd be bodies all over the place."

"Man, I've been on vacations tougher than this!" another Marine said with a laugh.

"Stay alert and don't get cocky," Sergeant Meredith said, cutting through the chatter. "You don't want to die laughing."

That shut them all up.

Up and down the beach, sergeants and lieutenants pulled squads and companies together out of the chaos. Ray and Big John and the sergeant were a part of "Easy Company," the nickname for Company E. Ray's squad came together, and they tiptoed their way up to the top of the dunes at the edge of the beach. There was nothing beyond that except for a patchwork of farms as far as the eye could see.

"Looks like you're getting that nickname after all, kid," Big John said, and Ray smiled in spite of himself. What was supposed to have been a meat grinder had been a cake walk instead. His pack was suddenly light as air, and he felt like he could march for days.

"Well heck, I already lived longer than I thought I would, so I'm happy!" said Private First Class Billy

Lineker, a redheaded nineteen-year-old from Fort Mill, South Carolina. Everybody called him "Hardluck" Lineker because he'd been shot in the butt at Peleliu and recovered just in time to get himself sent to Okinawa.

"I never heard of this Okinawa place until a couple of weeks ago," said Private Francisco Gonzalez. He hailed from Visalia, California, and, though he wasn't as big and burly as Big John, he was the squad's other BAR gunner. Like Ray, he was a new recruit. "Why we even want it?"

"We've been playing leapfrog through the Pacific," explained Corporal Travis Starks. Everybody called Starks "The Old Man" because he was twenty-four and married with twin daughters back home in Lee's Summit, Missouri. "Island to island to island. This is the last rock before the jump to Japan. We take Okinawa, and it's next stop Tokyo."

"This *is* Japan, technically speaking," said Sergeant Meredith. "Even though it's its own island, with its own people, it's still a prefecture of Japan. Like one of our states back home. And don't think the Japs are gonna give it up without a fight."

Everyone nodded, and Ray's pack started to feel a little heavier.

"All right, we gotta hump half a click east by nightfall to secure the area around the landing beach,"

Sergeant Meredith said. Ray knew that this meant they had to march east with all their gear for half a kilometer.

"Half a click by nightfall?" the Old Man said. "That's crazy. If Okinawa is anything like Peleliu, there'll be caves full of Japanese soldiers all over the place. We won't get a hundred yards before we're pinned down."

"Our orders are half a click by nightfall, so we make it half a click by nightfall," Sergeant Meredith said firmly. He showed them a map of the immediate area. "Easy Company will spread out here, along this road, heading east. The rest of the First Marines will hump it north above us, and the Army's 96th Division will flank us on the right and then make a hard right turn south. Time's a-wasting. Let's move out."

Ray's squad got walking down a dirt road through some of the prettiest countryside he'd ever seen. Neat little fields grew rice and beans and sweet potatoes and sugarcane. Thatch-roofed farmhouses sat nestled among forests of pine and bamboo and some kind of strange tree that Ray had never seen before. It had a dozen trunks instead of one, and a big round canopy on top with vines growing straight down like the stingers on a jellyfish.

In the distance, the farms rolled up into bright green hills and mountains. All in all, it could have been paradise if they hadn't been there to fight the Japanese. But there was something else wrong with it too, and finally Ray put his finger on it.

There weren't any people. Yes, he could see other rifle squads from Easy Company to the left and right, working their way cautiously through fields and forests. But there wasn't a single Okinawan around. Where had they all gone? Had they all been evacuated by the Japanese?

"Hey, look here!" Hard-luck Lineker cried, breaking the silence. They were passing by another farm and he pointed. "A pig!"

Sure enough, whoever had worked this farm had gone so quickly they'd left behind what looked like a year-old pig. Ray's squad collected at the fence to its pen to watch it snuffling around in the muck.

"Man, I ain't had a good pork chop in ages," Big John moaned.

"We ought to kill it and cook it up!" said Gonzalez.

They all looked to the sergeant, expecting a no, but he was licking his lips. "I'm right there with you, boys, but I'm a plumber. I don't know nothing about slaughtering any pig. Anybody else?"

They all shook their heads except for Ray. A horrible moment from a few years ago on the farm flashed through his mind, and he looked away, trying to forget. Slaughtering this pig would bring up a lot of bad memories for him. But the boys wanted it so bad, and Ray was so eager to earn their friendship.

"I do," Ray said at last. "We used to do it every year back on the farm."

His squad mates' eyes went wide, and suddenly Ray was the most popular guy on all of Okinawa.

"What do you say, Sergeant?"

"Can we do it?"

Sergeant Meredith thought on it. "Well, we're already way ahead of schedule. And I'd sure like me some ribs."

The other men of Ray's squad hooted and hollered and slapped him and the sergeant on their backs. "All right, all right," Sergeant Meredith said. "Don't make too much noise about it, or the other squads'll hear and want a taste."

Hard-luck climbed up on the fence to go over into the pen after the pig.

Pak! Something popped in the distance, and suddenly Hard-luck Lineker looked confused. His head dropped to his chest, where a dark liquid was spreading across the front of his uniform. He wobbled and fell over forward. Ray didn't understand what was going on until Big John tackled him.

"Get down! Get down!" Sergeant Meredith cried. "Sniper!"

HIDEKI

BLOOD AND IRON

THOOM.

Hideki flinched, but he didn't run. He sat in the safety of a cave, watching through its entrance as American shells exploded over the next hill. He could feel the vibrations deep inside the island's bedrock.

Hideki and the other boys had made their way down to the beaches, intending to seek out the Americans. But the constant shelling from the ships in the harbor had driven them away, and they'd sought shelter inside one of Okinawa's many natural caves.

The rest of the boys were deeper inside, talking and laughing. Hideki would have joined them, but Yoshio was there, and it always paid to stay as far away from Yoshio as possible—even if that meant being closer to the American bombs.

Hideki sucked on a piece of *kanpan*, a tough dried biscuit. He hated to already eat what little food the army had given him, but he was hungry. And besides, the Imperial Japanese Army was going to drive the Americans from the island in a matter of days, weren't they? If everything went the way the IJA promised, the battle would be over soon. Then Hideki's mother and brother would come home from Japan, and his father and sister would come home from the front lines. The whole family would be together again.

It had been almost eight months since his mother and little brother, Isamu, went away. Since Hideki too was *supposed* to go away. He still remembered that day as though he had a picture of it. The hot August sun, the narrow docks, the throngs of Okinawans pressing toward the big black passenger ships waiting to take them north to mainland Japan.

Hideki's mother carried Isamu in her arms, and Isamu clutched his little papier-mâché lion-dog. Hideki followed behind with his father and his older sister, Kimiko.

"You'll be safe in Japan. Yes, much safer than on Okinawa," Hideki's father said, as though he was trying to convince himself too. Otō was short, like Hideki, but stocky, with a mustache and a trim black beard. He stood next to Hideki's sister, who was already taller than both their mother and father. Kimiko was thin and elegant, with a white streak in her long black hair that had marked her since she was little as a *yuta*—a person who could see and speak to the dead. Otō and Kimiko were there to say good-bye, not go with them. Otō had already been drafted into the IJA to fight, and Kimiko had been taken from her school and pressed into service as a nurse in an army hospital.

Hideki hugged his sister and his father, his heart aching. His family had never been apart before. He hated to leave them, but he hurried to join his mother and little brother so Kimiko and his father couldn't see his tears.

He was almost on board the ship when someone grabbed him roughly by the arm.

"Here, what's this?" demanded a scowling Japanese soldier. He held Hideki back. "Just where do you think you're going? How old are you?"

"Thirteen," Hideki said, surprised. "Almost fourteen."

"Fourteen is old enough to fight!" the soldier barked.

Kimiko stepped between them. "You don't understand," she told the soldier. "Hideki's a scaredy-cat. Three hundred and fifty years ago, one of our ancestors died like a coward, and now every third generation the oldest boy is born afraid. This time around it's Hideki. Until our ancestor's spirit finds peace, he's worthless in a fight."

Hideki's face burned red with embarrassment, but everything his sister said was true.

"Superstitious *dojin*," the soldier muttered, and Hideki heard his father gasp. *Dojin* was a rude way of saying "primitive natives." The soldier was basically calling them animals.

Hideki's fists tightened around the sack of clothes he carried. He *was* a coward. But it wasn't his fault. He was just born that way. And no amount of ceremonies and offerings to his ancestor had been able to free him from it.

Maybe, he thought, it was time to try a more direct approach. Maybe it was time to override his ancestor's cowardice with his own bravery.

Hideki stood tall. "I'm going to stay," he announced.

His father and sister protested, but there was no time, and they couldn't make him go. His mother and little brother were swept up the ramp by the surging crowds, and Hideki waved good-bye to them. The Japanese soldier nodded his approval at Hideki and went to harass someone else.

Kimiko smacked Hideki on the back of his head. "Idiot," she told him.

Kimiko's rebuke echoed in Hideki's mind now as the shelling from the American battleships abruptly stopped. The silence was startling. There could only be one reason the Americans weren't shooting anymore, Hideki realized—because they were afraid of hitting their own soldiers. That meant there had to be Americans close by!

The bushes outside the cave rustled, and Hideki's breath caught in his throat. He pulled one of his ceramic grenades from his jacket pocket and removed the rubber cap. He wished he had one of the real grenades, the kind where you just pulled a safety pin to activate it. He held the striking cap close to the fuse, his hands shaking.

"Wh-who goes there?" Hideki called, trying his best to hide the fear in his voice.

People emerged from the bushes, and Hideki relaxed. It was an Okinawan family—an old woman, a mother with a baby in her arms, and a girl much younger than Hideki who clung to her mother's dress.

"You must let us in, please," the mother said, trying to keep her voice down. "There are Americans all around us. We can't let them capture us." She pulled her children closer. The old woman's face was streaked with tears.

"Come on in, then! Hurry!" Hideki told them.

Yoshio and some of the other boys had noticed that the bombing had stopped, and they came to the mouth of the cave to see what was happening. As soon as he saw the Okinawan family trying to come inside, Yoshio blocked their way.

"Where do you think you're going?" Yoshio said. "You can't come in here. This is a military cave."

Hideki wanted to argue—wasn't it the army's job to

protect the people of Okinawa? But he didn't want Yoshio to turn on him again.

"Go away!" Yoshio told the family.

"Yes," Hideki said, brandishing his grenade to show them he meant business. "This cave belongs to the Blood and Iron Student Corps. Go hide somewhere else."

A strange noise came from the other side of the hill. A motorized rumbling like the sound of a bus.

The women and children heard it too, and they turned and ran away, screaming. Hideki's heart raced, and his stomach twisted. Was this it for real? Had some of the Americans gotten past the beach? Was he finally going to have to fight?

"Hideki, go see what it is," Yoshio said. He shoved Hideki with both hands, and Hideki stumbled outside into the harsh daylight.

Be brave like the kamikazes, Hideki reminded himself. Grenade in one hand, rubber striking cap in the other, he took a deep breath and ducked into the bushes at the top of the hill. He crept forward until he could see over the ridge.

The dirt path below him was lined with American vehicles. Gray trucks filled with soldiers. Enormous clanking green things with cannons on top and treads for wheels. Open-topped jeeps pulling giant guns on trailers. There were scores of them. They kept coming around the bend in the road. And kept coming and coming.

Hideki ducked deeper into the thicket, afraid they would see him. His hands shook. How was this possible? How had the American devils been able to get so many vehicles past the Japanese defenses? Hideki had seen more automobiles on that road in five minutes than there had been in all of Okinawa before the war.

Hideki's shaking fear crystallized into a hard knot in his stomach, and he knew what he had to do. He had to take out one of those trucks with a grenade. This was his moment. This was his fate. He stood up, fully exposed if any of the soldiers in the trucks had bothered to look up at him, and got ready to strike the match-like fuse on his grenade.

For the Emperor, Hideki told himself. *For Japan. For my family.*

Hands grabbed Hideki and pulled him back into the bushes before he could activate his grenade. Hideki turned around. It was Yoshio!

"What are you doing?!" Hideki cried.

"The Americans—they're close by!" Yoshio told him.

"I know! The road down there is full of them!"

"No, you fathead. Closer than that!" Yoshio said. "One of the boys heard somebody crashing through the forest, and we're all going to attack!"

RAY

PIGS TO THE SLAUGHTER

"Down! Down! Sniper!" Starks yelled.

Ray scrambled under the wooden fence that kept the pig inside. *Pak!*—another bullet hit right where he'd been lying two seconds ago.

Ray flattened himself in the mud. There was a ridge underneath the fence that was just tall enough to hide behind, but no more. He held his helmet with both hands as the rest of his squad crawled under the fence and flopped into the muck beside him.

"What about Hard-luck?" Starks asked. There was barely room for all five of them behind the little ridge.

"Dead," Sergeant Meredith answered. He unlatched the bayonet from his rifle, balanced his helmet on top of the bayonet, and slowly raised his rifle above the ridge line.

Pak! The sound of the sniper's rifle was quickly followed by the sound of the bullet hitting the helmet. *Pang!* Ray watched the helmet tumble toward the pig, who was still snuffling away on the other side of the pen. Ray saw the hole where the bullet had gone clean through the helmet. He swallowed hard.

"Dang. That guy's good," Gonzalez said.

"Wait—*shhhh*," the sergeant said. He waved them all quiet, and over the sound of the pig grunting, Ray heard a sound he recognized from his hunting days.

"Bolt action," Ray whispered.

Sergeant Meredith nodded, and Ray felt a quick lick of pride, like he'd answered a question right in class.

"He has to manually chamber a new round every time he fires," the sergeant said. "That gives us a chance. You think you'd recognize that sound again?" he asked Ray.

Ray nodded.

"All right. Gonzalez, Big John, get those BARs ready to go. Ray, next time that sniper shoots, I want you to get over that fence and run to that well on the other side of the road. We'll lay down cover fire for you. You hide there, and the next time you hear that bolt action, you chuck a grenade at it. Got it?"

Run across an open road with a sniper out there? Ray's breath came quick. He felt lightheaded, but he nodded. He wriggled out of his pack, pushed his helmet down on his head again, and gripped his M-1 rifle so hard his knuckles turned white.

He would do it. He *had* to do it. This was what he'd signed on for, after all. Why he'd left his home in Nebraska.

He remembered how his father had argued with him, forbidden him to go.

"You've got a deferment from the government!" his father had shouted. "You don't have to go, and we still need you on the farm."

"I just—I gotta do my part before the war ends," Ray had told him.

There hadn't been a whipping this time. Ray was too old for that. It was hypocritical for his Pa to protest anyway, and they both knew it. Ray's father had done the same thing when he was Ray's age—run off to join the Marines to fight in the Great War.

And they both knew the real reason Ray had wanted to leave home. The long scar on his left arm peeking out from his shirt sleeve was all the reminder Ray needed.

Pak! A bullet hit the mud with a *thwack* a half an inch from Big John's boot.

"Jumpin' Jehosephat!" Big John yelled, wiggling his legs up closer to him. But Ray was already leaping over the fence. His feet hit the ground with a thump and he ran like blue blazes for the protection of the stone well across the road. The well had appeared closer before, but now it looked like it was half a mile away.

Stay low. Run like hell.

Behind him, Gonzalez and Big John opened up with their big Browning Automatics to create cover fire for Ray. *Chu-chu-chung! Chu-chu-chu-chu-chung!* The guns chewed the ferns and palm fronds along the bank into shreds. Ray stumbled but kept his feet, desperately trying to remember how long it had been since the last sniper shot. Three seconds? Four? How long did it take him to chamber a new bullet after he'd taken a shot at a deer?

Ray made it across the dirt road and threw himself at the base of the round well. The BARs stopped firing. Ray's chest heaved, and he struggled to catch his breath. No time to rest though. He dropped his rifle and fumbled for a grenade, his hands shaking. He wondered if the sniper had even seen him through all that cover fire.

Pa-kow! A piece of the well's stone wall blew up in Ray's face, and he ducked away. That answered that question. The sniper rifle's report was much louder now, much closer. Ray popped up, heart in his throat, and strained to listen for the sound of the rifle's bolt sliding back and forth. He was totally exposed standing there, and Gonzalez and Big John couldn't fire again to cover him, or he wouldn't be able to hear the sound of the bolt.

Ch-chik.

There! Ray picked a spot in the trees he thought the sound had come from, pulled the pin, and threw his grenade toward the green hillside. He dropped down and grabbed his helmet to his head.

KA-THOOM! The hillside above him exploded, showering everything with dirt and rocks and plants.

"Hands in the air! Stay where you are!" Sergeant Meredith yelled.

Ray grabbed his rifle and peeked out from behind the well. The sniper had tumbled out of the ground cover on the hill and was just getting to his feet. Ray hadn't hit him, but he'd flushed him from hiding.

Rifle raised, Ray got to his feet and ran at the Japanese soldier—or was he Okinawan? He wasn't wearing a uniform and didn't have any other equipment.

"Dang, he's just a kid," the Old Man said as the others ran up.

He *was* a kid, Ray realized. He was cowering and sniffling like he'd gotten in trouble. He couldn't have been more than twelve years old.

"Well, there's your first Jap," Big John told Ray.

"I think he's Okinawan," said Ray.

"If he was shooting at us, he's a Jap," Big John said.

"So, do we take him prisoner?" Ray asked. "I've got my Japanese phrase book—"

Sergeant Meredith shook his head. "We can't take prisoners, kid. We have to keep moving."

Ray didn't understand. "But what about the support services for Okinawans?"

"That's for refugees," the sergeant told him. "He's an enemy combatant."

"You want to do the honors?" Big John asked Ray. "You flushed him out."

Ray still didn't understand what was going on, and Sergeant Meredith shook his head at Big John.

Big John shrugged, pulled out his pistol, and shot the boy. Ray almost jumped out of his boots, but only Gonzalez flinched with him. The others, the ones who'd been together at Peleliu and beyond, they didn't bat an eye.

Big John put his pistol back in its holster and clapped Ray on the shoulder. "Now," he said, "let's take Hard-luck's body back, and get you to cooking up that pig."

HIDEKI

MABUI

Hideki's hands were so sweaty he worried the grenade he held would slip right out of his grasp. He wiped a hand on his jacket and nodded to Katsumasa, who was a few yards to his left. All the boys were hiding behind whatever bushes and tree trunks hadn't been destroyed by the offshore bombardment. As a group they crept forward, drawing closer to where they had heard some-one crashing through the undergrowth.

Hideki strained to catch every sound, every move-ment. Yoshio waved for everyone to stop, and then Hideki heard it—the crunch and snap of heavy footfalls on the forest floor. Someone was coming! The footsteps got louder, more urgent, and Hideki heard a man's breath.

This is it, he thought. *This is my moment of glory.* But Hideki didn't feel glorious. His stomach was tied up in knots and he could barely breathe. He wasn't even sure he could stand.

One of the boys jumped out from where he was hiding and yelled "*Banzai!*" and more of them did the same. Hideki borrowed some of their courage and leaped to his feet, ready to strike the fuse on his grenade and throw it at an American soldier.

But it wasn't an American soldier. Huffing along the trail was Norio Kojima, their school principal! The portly man's uniform was muddy and torn, and he hugged a tall canvas sack to his chest.

Principal Kojima cried out in surprise as the boys all popped up screaming and brandishing grenades, and he tripped over his own feet and fell to the ground. The sack broke his fall, but something inside it shattered and snapped. Framed pictures spilled out onto the forest floor.

"No—no!" the principal cried.

"Principal Kojima?" Hideki said. Luckily, none of the boys had activated their grenades, and now they all hurried to help their principal to his feet.

"The Emperor—the pictures of the Emperor!" Kojima said. "Some of them have been damaged!"

Hideki picked up one of the framed photographs that was still intact. It was a picture of Emperor Hirohito. A portrait of the Emperor hung in every room at school. Hideki and the other boys had to bow to the picture and the Japanese flag every time they came or went. Principal Kojima must have collected every one of the portraits and stuffed them into this sack.

Principal Kojima scrambled to collect the other pictures. "It is my sacred duty to protect the Divine Emperor's photographs!" he said. "I'm taking these north to the Imperial Photograph Guardian Unit. The Emperor's spirit must be protected!"

Hideki had never seen Principal Kojima so frantic, and it scared him a little. He could tell the other boys were frightened too. But Hideki understood the principal's concern. A person's spirit, what the Okinawans called "*mabui*," was like his soul. It's what made you who you were. Everybody had a *mabui*, including Hideki. A *mabui* was immortal, and transferable. A ring you inherited from your grandmother might have her *mabui* in it. A watch your father had owned might still carry his *mabui*. You could even lose your *mabui* if you weren't careful. And pictures, whether they were drawings or photographs like these of Emperor Hirohito, they carried part of a person's *mabui* in them too. So it was like each of these photos was a little piece of the Emperor's soul.

It was the *mabui* of Hideki's cowardly ancestor, Shigetomo Kaneshiro, that still cursed every third generation of Hideki's family. Hideki's own *mabui* shared space inside him with the spirit of Shigetomo. As long as Shigetomo's spirit was still restless, Hideki would never know peace, and could never truly be himself.

Hideki's sister had tried to help him with Shigetomo's *mabui* in her official role as a *yuta*. But Kimiko had always had more success with other people. Once, Hideki remembered, he had gone with her on a house call to a family with a young boy who kept getting in trouble at school. That day Kimiko had worn a white *bashōfu*, a lightweight banana-fiber kimono, that matched the streak in her hair.

"Shinsei keeps getting into fights!" the boy's mother had complained. "I have to bring him home at least once a week. His older brother, Ichiro, never got into trouble like this!"

Shinsei was a scruffy, surly boy of seven with a thin trickle of snot running down his dirty face. Hideki thought he looked like trouble, but Kimiko smiled at the boy and talked to him like an adult.

"Have you been having bad dreams, Shinsei?" she asked him.

Shinsei frowned and looked away. In the next room, a baby cried, and Shinsei's mother got up to see to it.

"Shinsei?" Kimiko tried again.

"Yes," the boy grunted. "A female wolf comes and chases me out of the house and won't let me back in."

"I think I understand," Kimiko said.

"You do?" Shinsei asked.

"*You do?*" Hideki asked. He was confused. None of it made any sense to him.

"The wolf in Shinsei's dream represents a female ancestor born in the year of the dog," Kimiko explained. When Shinsei's mother came back, Kimiko asked her if there was someone matching that description who had been a troublemaker in the past.

"Yes, my Aunt Toshi!" the mother said. "My mother's middle sister. She was always running around with boys my grandfather didn't like. Oh, the fights they would have."

Kimiko nodded. "Shinsei has his Great-Aunt Toshi's *mabui* on him. She's still acting out through him. Go once a week to the family tomb where she is buried—just the two of you—and perform the ceremony I teach you."

"You got all that from his dream about a wolf?" Hideki asked later as he and Kimiko walked home.

Kimiko grinned. "Well, not all of it. Being a *yuta* is about listening to our ancestors, but it's about paying attention to the living too. Did you hear the cries from the other room? There's a new baby in the house. And his mother mentioned an *older* brother, which makes Shinsei the middle child. The oldest brother has all the responsibility, and the baby gets all the mother's attention. Shinsei doesn't have a role in the family anymore, so he acts out to get any kind of attention, even if it's negative attention. He probably doesn't even know he's doing it. But now he and his mother will spend time together once a week walking back and forth to the family tomb to perform a ceremony together, and Shinsei will get lots of attention without having to get into trouble."

"So . . . all that about his Great-Aunt Toshi, you just made that up?" Hideki asked.

Kimiko smacked him on the head. "No! Her *mabui* really is on him. She was a middle child too, didn't you hear? She probably went through the same thing, only there was no *yuta* to send her on long walks to the family tomb with her mother, so she never got over it." Kimiko's voice grew quiet. "I hope Shinsei's trips to the family tomb with his mother will bring both him *and* his Great-Aunt Toshi peace in the end."

Hideki still had trouble understanding it all, but his sister seemed to know what she was talking about.

"I'm a middle child too, and I never acted like that," he'd said at last.

"That's because you have a different *mabui* to worry about," Kimiko told him.

One Hideki would have to wait a little longer to appease.

"I've got to get these pictures to safety," Principal Kojima was saying now. Hideki watched as he stuffed the last of the Emperor's portraits back in the bag and stood up. "Remember to fight and die for your country with honor. We'll meet again in the afterlife!" he told his former students, and ran off.

The boys were debating whether to return to the cave or to keep looking for American soldiers when Yoshio perked up. "Do you smell that?" he whispered.

A delicious aroma tickled Hideki's nose, and he turned into the wind and sniffed. Somebody nearby was cooking something over a campfire. Something *good.* Hideki hadn't eaten meat in ages—all the meat in Okinawa now went to the Japanese soldiers—and his mouth watered at the tasty smell. Some of the other boys had picked up on it too, and they smiled at each other.

Hideki's stomach growled eagerly, but he didn't smile. The smell of roasting meat could mean only one thing.

"Americans," he whispered.

RAY

BARBECUE

Ray sat apart from the other Marines, watching them laugh and talk as they ate barbecued pig. His squad had met up with the rest of Easy Company—strength in numbers as they set up camp for the night. From the safety of their foxholes, they were all sharing in the feast Ray had prepared. He was the man of the hour, but he didn't feel much like celebrating. He'd just watched Billy Lineker get shot in front of him. So had the other men in Ray's squad. How could they be joking and enjoying barbecue just a few hours later?

Sergeant Meredith sat down on the edge of Ray's foxhole. "You did good today," Sergeant Meredith said. "Flushing that sniper out."

Flushing that twelve-year-old boy out, Ray thought. *That little kid.*

"You okay with it?" the sergeant asked.

"The sniper? I guess," Ray said. As surprising as it was that the sniper was just a kid, Ray understood why they'd had to kill him. This was a war. It was kill or be killed, and the kid had killed one of theirs. But the way Big John had done it, so easily. So casually . . .

But that wasn't even what was bothering him the most about that day.

"And Hard-luck?" Sergeant Meredith said, as though he could read Ray's mind.

Ray huffed. "I don't understand." He raised his chin at the other men. "Don't they care?"

"They do care, yes," said the sergeant. "So do I. But it's fate—either you have a bullet or a mortar or a grenade with your name on it, or you don't. That bullet finds you and we mourn, but we have to move on. Nothing else we *can* do."

"But it just seems so—so heartless," Ray said.

"It is," Sergeant Meredith allowed. "But Marines like me and Big John and the Old Man, this ain't our first rodeo. We've seen a lot of good men die. If we mourned every one of them the way they should be mourned, we'd go crazy." The sergeant rubbed a callus on his palm—the same place Ray's rifle had given him blisters during basic training. "We had to let our skins harden up, so we don't feel it as much. We can't, or it'd hurt too bad. You ever see a guy with that thousand-yard stare? You know it's getting to him."

Ray had seen that stare before in his father's eyes, like he was focused on something a long way off that nobody else could see. Ray knew that's when his Pa had been remembering his time in the First World War. Over in his foxhole, the Old Man was doing it now.

"Starks, grab me a hunk of that pig, will you?" Sergeant Meredith called to him.

The Old Man shook himself out of the stare and grinned. "Sure, Sergeant."

Sergeant Meredith glanced at Ray, and Ray understood.

Their lieutenant found them and told Sergeant Meredith that scouts had reported a possible enemy cave nearby. "Send a team to check it out while we've still got some daylight," the lieutenant said.

The sergeant saluted and called Big John over. "Big John, take Gonzalez and Barbecue here and a couple of the other rookies and show 'em the ropes."

And just like that, Ray had a nickname: Barbecue.

The cave was a quarter of a mile away from camp, very close to a steep cliff that ran a long way down to the sea, where waves crashed against big rocks. It was a natural cavern, with rock walls and a dirt floor. The entrance was about half as tall as Ray and overgrown with moss. It was pitch-black just a foot or two inside. There was no telling how far it went back into the hill-side, or if anybody was hiding inside.

"Is someone going in there?" Gonzalez asked.

"You kiddin'?" Big John said. "We're gonna flush 'em out. Rifles ready."

Big John took a grenade from his belt, pulled the pin, and chucked it inside. Ray raised his rifle to his shoulder and aimed at the entrance.

THOOM. The explosion shook the ground, and smoke billowed out from the entrance. Inside, there were screams.

Ray's heart raced, and he shuffled his feet nervously. Suddenly, people came streaming out from the cave and Ray's finger tightened on the trigger. But it was a woman holding a baby. And the next target Ray swung to was a little boy. Then an old man.

"Wait—wait!" Ray cried. "They're Okinawans! Civilians!"

The Okinawans kept coming. Ten, fifteen, twenty—Ray lost count. He watched as the people ran away screaming from the Marines. They went straight for the edge of the cliff and raced back and forth along the edge of it, looking down like they were trying to find some path to escape. But Ray and the other Marines had walked along that ridge to get here—it was just a long fall into rocks and trees.

The grenade going off must have spooked them, Ray thought. He fished out his Japanese phrase book and tried to find something that would calm them down.

"Hee-DOY koat-o wa shee ma-SEN," he tried, walking closer. "We're not going to hurt you," he said in English.

The women and children wailed as Ray got closer, sobbing like it was the end of the world, and Ray wondered if he was saying it wrong.

Then the whole lot of them stepped off the cliff.

Ray blinked, and his stomach dropped. One second they had been huddled there in fear, and the next moment they were just gone.

"No!" Ray cried. There was no way they could have survived the fall.

"Jumpin' Jehoshaphat," Big John whispered.

"Why in the name of God would they do that?" Gonzalez asked.

None of them had the answer. Ray double-checked his phrase book—he hadn't said anything wrong. But for some reason the Okinawans had been so terrified of him and the other Marines that they had killed themselves rather than be captured.

"Well, better that than one of 'em coming out with a grenade and trying to blow us up," Big John said. "Let's make sure there ain't any more of 'em in there, and then get back and get us some more of that pig before it's gone."

Ray followed Big John into the cave, but he wouldn't be eating any more barbecue tonight. Ray had lost his appetite.

HIDEKI

BANZAI

Hideki and the other boys crept toward the delicious smell, and sure enough, there they were. American soldiers. There were almost twenty of them, sitting around a cook fire or in holes they had dug in the ground. Some of them wrote letters or cleaned their guns. Others were eating a pig they'd cooked up. Hideki could hear their voices on the breeze—the long, slow, deep, slurred sounds of English that made no sense to him.

None of the soldiers had seen or heard them yet, which meant the Blood and Iron Student Corps had the element of surprise. This really *was* Hideki's moment of glory, but he wasn't feeling so bold anymore. This was going to be a violent battle. This might be the moment he died.

One of the other boys, Takeshi, must have been

thinking the same thing too. Hideki could see him sobbing quietly a few meters away.

Shigetomo's *mabui* tugged at Hideki's gut, and Hideki took a step back.

"Here's what we'll do," Yoshio whispered at Hideki's side, making him jump. "We'll crawl closer, and then when we're all in range, I'll whistle, and—"

Ka-THOOM!

A grenade exploded close enough to knock them over, and Hideki's ears rang from the explosion.

"What—what happened?" he asked as he pulled himself back up on his knees.

"Takeshi killed himself! He blew himself up with his own grenade!" one of the boys yelled in horror.

Was it an accident, or had Takeshi killed himself out of fear? Hideki was still gaping, still trying to understand, when he heard the American soldiers cry out in alarm. The element of surprise was gone. The Americans were going for their guns! They would be on top of Hideki and the others in seconds.

"Attack! Attack!" Yoshio cried. He pulled the pin on his grenade, whacked the brass igniter on a rock, and hurled the grenade. It went off with a *POOM!* a few meters away. Hideki couldn't see what Yoshio had hit, because a second later the bullets started flying.

Pak pak pak pak! Chu-chu-chu-chung!

Hideki barely had room to curl up and hide behind a shredded tree stump. He watched as a fifth-year named Gensei couldn't get to cover in time. Gensei was hit again and again by bullets, his body dancing like a broken puppet before he crumpled to the ground.

Hideki had never seen somebody die before. His own body shook uncontrollably, like he was the one being hit, and tears sprang to his eyes.

"*Banzai!*" some of the boys cried, and Hideki heard one or two more grenades explode. The American bullets became a deadly hailstorm, and Hideki clenched himself into a tight, shaking ball. He looked at the grenade he held in his hand. He knew he should be brave. He knew he should stand up and throw his grenade and kill as many Americans as he could, the way Lieutenant Colonel Sano had told him to, but he couldn't do it. His fear froze him. He couldn't move.

Off to his right, his friend Katsumasa stood, grenade in hand. "Long live the Emperor!" he cried. Katsumasa threw his grenade with all his strength. The grenade hit a tree, bounced right back at Katsumasa, and exploded in his face with a *BOOM*.

The blast knocked Hideki from his hiding place, and he landed on his back with a thump that knocked the wind from him. He gasped for air and swallowed a scream. *This was a disaster.* It wasn't supposed to go like this. This wasn't what it had been like in training. It was all happening so *fast*, and they had no control over any of it.

Hideki was going to die here. They were all going to die here! His eyes darted around, looking for somewhere to hide, but all he saw was the decimated hillside. Less than half a dozen of the boys were still alive and fighting. The rest had been shot or blown apart. And if he didn't get out of here, Hideki was going to join them.

RAY

FIRST WATCH

Ray leaned on his entrenching tool and stretched his sore back. He'd spent the last half hour digging a four-foot-deep foxhole with Big John that both of them would sleep in that night. If he'd thought shoveling hay back home was hard, it was nothing compared to shoveling sand and coral on Okinawa.

Was this what it was like for my father in the First World War? Ray thought. That war had been all trenches and foxholes. Were his father's arms and back sore every night from digging endless ditches?

When the hole was finished, Ray wanted nothing more than to pass out in it and sleep until next week, but no such luck.

"Barbecue," the sergeant called. "You've got guard duty first watch. And be careful. While you two were off clearing caves, we were attacked by a bunch of kids with grenades."

Ray had heard the sound of shots and explosions in the distance as they'd been returning from the cave. He shook his head. Women and children throwing themselves off a cliff? Children with grenades? This definitely wasn't what he signed up for.

Big John clapped Ray on the shoulder. "The fun never stops when you're a Marine. Don't worry. I'll stay up with you for a bit."

Ray sighed and picked up his rifle.

"Don't forget this," Big John said, plunking Ray's helmet on his head. "That helmet's the best thing the Marine Corps ever gave you, Barbecue. It's got a hundred uses."

"Really?"

"Sure," Big John said. "You can wash in it, shave in it, cook coffee in it, and barf in it when you get sick. You can put gas in it to clean your gun, dig a hole with it if you lose your entrenching tool, sit on it, and use it to bail out your foxhole when it rains. That right there is the greatest military tool ever invented."

Ray reached up to straighten his helmet. "You forgot the part about it keeping you from getting shot in the head," he told Big John.

Big John snorted. "Oh, it don't do that."

Ray remembered the sniper putting a bullet right

through Sergeant Meredith's helmet. That made him think of Hard-luck again. The look on his face after the bullet hit him, the way he'd tumbled headfirst into the mud. Laughing and joking one minute, dead the next.

The camp settled into quiet as darkness fell. One man in each foxhole went to sleep while the others, like Ray, watched the surrounding terrain for intruders. But all Ray saw was Hard-luck, over and over again.

"How'd you end up in the Marines, Barbecue?" Big John whispered.

"Hunh?" Ray said, shaking off the memory of Hard-luck's death. Had Big John caught him doing the thousand-yard stare and asked him a question to distract him? It didn't matter. It had worked. "Oh, I, uh, I graduated from high school and I wasn't going to college, so I enlisted before I got drafted." He left out the part about the fight he'd had with his father. The awful things Ray had said to him. His mother in tears.

Big John nodded. "Me, I never finished eighth grade." He spoke quietly, just above a whisper, so they could hear any Japanese soldiers approaching. "I was already big enough to work and join a street gang, and that's what I did until I borrowed a car for a joyride and the cops got wise. Judge gave me a choice: join the Marines or go to juvie. Enlisting sounded a lot better than reform school, and here I am."

Ray couldn't believe Big John hadn't even finished

eighth grade—and that he'd been arrested for stealing a car! How many more of Easy Company had crazy stories about how they'd ended up in the Marines?

Something rustled in the undergrowth just beyond the camp's perimeter, and Big John put up a hand to tell Ray to be quiet. Ray raised his rifle and squinted in the half-light of the moon.

"How'd you make out, Joe?" asked a quiet voice. The words were English, but the accent was definitely Japanese. Before Ray knew what was happening, Big John opened up with his big Browning Automatic—*Chu-chu-chu-chu-chu*. Ray didn't know what Big John was shooting at until a Japanese soldier popped up right in front of them.

"*Banzai!*" the soldier screamed, charging Ray and Big John.

Ray flinched but pulled his trigger—*PAKOW*—and the bullet hit the soldier. He fell to the ground, but he wasn't dead yet. With the strength he still had left, the Japanese soldier raised his rifle in the direction of Big John. In a wild panic, Ray pointed his rifle straight down at the enemy soldier and shot him again—*PAKOW*—and at last the man was still.

Ray stood over the soldier, watching the life in his eyes go out.

More Marines from Easy Company came running

with their rifles, but it was all over as quickly as it had begun.

As his adrenaline wore off, Ray started to shake so much he couldn't stand. He staggered back, dropped his rifle, and collapsed inside the foxhole. He couldn't stop the tears that streamed from his eyes, and he turned away, sure Big John was going to make fun of him.

"Hey, it's okay, Ray," Big John said softly. He knelt beside Ray and put a hand on his shoulder. "I know what it feels like to kill a man for the first time," Big John told him. "We all do." That just made Ray cry harder. But it felt good to cry. To get it all out, all this sadness and terror and shaking rage he felt about everything he'd seen and done in just a day on Okinawa.

"You had to do it," Big John told him. "You saved us both."

Ray nodded, running his sleeve across his nose and wiping the tears from his eyes.

"It gets easier," Big John said, and Ray couldn't tell if he meant it as a good thing or a bad thing.

Big John stood. "Get your rifle and see if he's got anything on him."

Ray wiped his nose and dried his eyes again, and he stood. Looking at the body of the man he'd killed was easier if he didn't look at his face. Ray collected the soldier's rifle and laid it to his side. Then he went through the man's pockets. In one of them he found a wallet, and inside the wallet was a picture of the soldier and his family.

Ray was taken aback for a moment. Here was the face of the man he'd just killed, standing with a woman and a boy—probably his wife and young son. They all looked serious, the way people often did in old American photos. But the man had his hands on the shoulders of his wife and son. He loved them. Wanted to keep them safe.

Wanted to protect them from American devils like Ray.

Ray took the picture out of the wallet and put it in his pocket. Ray would keep the photo. Carry it with him. Keep this man and his family alive, in a way.

It felt like the right thing to do.

HIDEKI

HOW TO SURRENDER

Hideki cried as he ran. The forest around him blurred, but he kept running, stumbling blindly through the undergrowth.

No matter how far he ran, he couldn't escape his memories of what had happened. The whizzing bullets. The exploding grenades. Takeshi killing himself. Gensei, Katsumasa, all the other boys—dead. He didn't want to think it, didn't want to see it. But he couldn't *stop* seeing it. The images flashed in his mind faster than he could handle them.

Hideki tripped and fell, scraping his elbows. Heart in his throat, he felt for the ceramic grenades in his pocket, but neither of them had broken. As he got to his hands and knees, he saw that he'd tripped over a log. No, not a log, he realized—a *body*. He scrambled away from it, his heart racing, until he backed into a blasted tree stump. He was about to get up, to keep running, when he recognized the shape of the person through his tears.

"Principal Kojima?" Hideki asked. He sniffed and dragged his dirty sleeve across his eyes. The principal still clutched the sack full of pictures of the Emperor, but now he lay next to the sack, hugging it like a pillow.

Hideki approached slowly, cautiously, as though Principal Kojima might pop up and begin scolding him for speaking Okinawan and not Japanese. But Principal Kojima was dead—killed by the blast from an artillery shell. His face looked more concerned than pained. Even in death he was still worrying about protecting the Emperor's pictures.

Hideki pulled out one of the pictures and looked at it. His Majesty the Emperor was a young man, with a long nose, short mustache, and round, frameless glasses. He wore a ceremonial military uniform, with fancy braids on the shoulders and arms, a silk sash across the front, and so many medals that they filled the whole front of the jacket. Hideki felt a swell of pride for his country. Principal Kojima had been doing a brave thing, protecting His Majesty's *mabui.*

Maybe Hideki could make up for his own cowardice by taking over this sacred duty and seeing the photographs to safety.

Hideki repacked the photographs in the bag and found that Principal Kojima had a bit of bread and a sock full of rice tucked away too. That would come in handy.

An airplane roared overhead, and Hideki looked up. It wasn't a kamikaze—it was an American plane. And it was dropping something!

Hideki threw himself on the sack to protect it from the falling bombs. He put his hands over his head and clenched, waiting for the booms, but they didn't come. He heard a soft rustling instead.

Hideki looked up to see thousands of white pieces of paper fluttering to the ground like the cherry blossoms that fell from the *sakura* trees every spring.

The Americans were dropping paper?

Hideki caught a piece of paper and looked at it. It had Japanese writing on it. HOW TO SURRENDER it said in big, bold letters, and after that it explained how the Okinawans should approach American soldiers if they wanted to give themselves up and be protected. To make it clear you were surrending, the leaflet said, you should stay away from the Japanese army, leave the combat area immediately, and wear something white if possible.

Surrender? Hideki crumpled up the leaflet and threw it to the ground. It was like the Americans knew he was a coward and were teasing him about it. He wasn't going to surrender. And he wasn't going to let the Americans *or* Shigetomo's *mabui* tell him what to do.

Almost in response, the American battleships began to range in on his location. *Ka-THOOM. Ka-THOOM. Ka-THOOM.* The bombs were getting closer every second. Hideki quickly hefted the sack onto his shoulders. He had to get away from here. But where?

Hideki's mind went to the safest place he could think of: his *haka*, his family's tomb. *Yes.* It wasn't far. Hideki put his head down and ran through the falling bombs, zigging and zagging so they couldn't catch him. When he was clear of the artillery, he kept running, past the crater-filled rice paddies and burned-down farmhouses outside his village. He had been to his family tomb so many times in his life he knew the way by heart.

The Kaneshiros' *haka* was where they buried their dead. It was where they came to worship and celebrate them too. Going back to it felt like going home, in a way, and gave Hideki a new sense of confidence and purpose. Three times a year, Hideki helped his father clean the tomb. Eventually, the job would be his, until he could share the duty with his own firstborn son.

Where was his father now? Hideki wondered. Was he alive? Was he dead? He might never know.

As he rounded the last turn to his family tomb, Hideki worried that it might not be there anymore. That an American bomb might have blasted it and all of Hideki's ancestors to bits. But there it was, just as it had always been, and his heart soared.

The Kaneshiro *haka* was built into a hill and had a big round roof that resembled a giant turtle shell. Family name markers sat in the courtyard outside.

The small door to the tomb was fronted by a narrow porch with a railing. If he looked through the frame of his fingers, Hideki could see the porch as it had been before—his extended family gathered to make their annual offerings of incense, food, and rice liquor to their ancestors and share the happy feast with the spirits. It was one of the days Hideki most looked forward to, but they had missed it this year. Everyone had been relocated by the Japanese army or was too busy working for them. Or both.

The most recent time he'd been back here was with Kimiko. He and his sister had come over the winter to repeat the ritual they hoped would finally bring peace to Shigetomo, and free Hideki from the influence of his ancestor's *mabui*. Kimiko had noticed that Hideki was moving stiffly as they prepared the incense and offerings for the ceremony, and she pulled back the sleeve of his shirt to reveal the bruises on his arm he'd been trying to hide.

"Who did this to you?" Kimiko demanded.

Hideki looked at the floor. "Yoshio," he said. "A boy at school."

"Did you at least fight back?" Kimiko asked.

"No! Yoshio would have beaten me up!"

Kimiko smacked Hideki in the head. "He *did* beat you up. And he'll keep doing it until you stand up to him."

"It's Shigetomo's fault," Hideki told her. "He makes me scared."

Kimiko shook her head. "It's not about being scared," she told him. "It's about doing what you have to do, *even though* you're scared." She yanked Hideki's sleeve back down to hide his bruises again. She was still frowning, but her tone softened. "If he does it again, come and get me and *I'll* beat him up."

Hideki could never do that—let his sister fight bullies for him? The boys at school would never let him live that down! But he still hadn't stood up to Yoshio either. Kimiko just didn't understand.

Hideki crawled inside the dark tomb just as it began to rain outside. He suddenly realized he might not be the first person to think of hiding out here, and he called out in Japanese.

"Hello? Is anyone here?"

He repeated his question in Okinawan, despite his fears that someone Japanese might overhear him and punish him for speaking his native language. When the Japanese had taken over Okinawa all those years ago, they'd made it illegal for the Okinawans to speak their own language or practice their own religion.

"Hideki?" said a weak voice, and Hideki froze.

Goose bumps crawled up and down his arms. Were his ancestors speaking to him? Was this the voice of Shigetomo, the ancestor whose *mabui* he carried?

"Hideki, is that you?" the voice croaked again.

It *was* an ancestor, Hideki realized with a start. But not one nearly so old as Shigetomo.

"Otō!" Hideki cried. It was his father.

RAY

FIRE IN THE HOLE

"I'm coming out!" Ray called. He didn't want his rifle squad to shoot him as he exited the little Okinawan tomb. Sergeant Meredith, Big John, and the others waited outside, rifles at the ready, as Ray ducked through the doorway.

Rain poured down on Ray like he was standing under the well-pump back home. He leaned against the outside of the tomb, trying not to lose his breakfast.

"Empty?" Big John asked.

"It is now," Ray said. After a Marine had chucked a grenade inside the tomb, Sergeant Meredith had sent Ray inside to see if there was anyone still alive.

There wasn't. Not anymore. There had been—an Okinawan family had been hiding among the ceramic pots that held their ancestors. But they were gone now.

The grenade had destroyed both the living *and* the dead.

Ray put the back of his hand to his mouth, but he wasn't going to be sick. As horrible as it was in there, he'd seen worse already.

God help me, I'm getting used to it, Ray thought. Just like Big John had said. But Ray didn't want to get used to it. That was how you became heartless like Big John, or stared off into the distance like the Old Man. Or like Ray's father. Ray didn't ever want sights like this to sit easy with him.

"Let's move out," Sergeant Meredith told his squad.

"Sergeant, wait," Ray said. "That tomb, it was full of Okinawans. Women and children. We gotta stop using grenades on them."

"But the last tomb was full of Japs," Big John reminded him. "They had built a machine gun nest into it!"

"I know, but sometimes there's innocent people in there," Ray argued. "We should at least be using smoke grenades on them. That won't kill them. Just flush them out."

"Yeah, flush 'em out shooting," said Big John.

"Dang it, Majors, that's just what the Japs want us to do!" said Private First Class Brown, a rifleman from another squad.

Sergeant Meredith grabbed PFC Brown by the

poncho and slammed him up against the stone wall of the tomb. "You don't *ever* call that boy by his last name again," the sergeant barked. "Do you understand me, Private?"

Sergeant Meredith thrust Brown up against the tomb once more, knocking loose his helmet. Rain poured down on the private's head as he nodded, his eyes scared.

Sergeant Meredith turned on the rest of the squad, and they all took a step back. "It's *Ray*, or it's *Barbecue*. But never *Majors*. Do you understand me? The next joker who says it gets nicknamed 'General.'"

Another Marine snorted at the idea of a death wish for a nickname, and Sergeant Meredith let go of Brown and glared at him. "You think I'm kidding?"

Everybody found somewhere else to look.

"We use smoke grenades on the tombs from here on out," Sergeant Meredith told them. "We don't none of us wear this uniform because it's easy."

There was some grumbling at the decision, but Sergeant Meredith was the boss. He gave them fifteen minutes before they had to head out again, and Ray found a place to be alone. The sergeant had yelled at everybody on his behalf, and Ray was the reason they couldn't chuck frag grenades in tombs anymore. Ray wasn't the most popular guy in the squad right now, and he could feel it.

Ray found shelter under a palm frond and took the

pictures he'd collected out of his pack. After he'd taken the first photograph from the man he'd killed with his rifle, it had become something Ray did after every encounter. Now he had pictures of families, pictures of sweethearts, pictures of houses and pets and parents. They weren't all from Japanese soldiers he'd killed himself, but a lot of them were.

"Why do you keep all them things?" Big John asked, making Ray jump. He hadn't heard him come up.

"I don't know," Ray said. "Don't you wonder about these people? Who they are? Where they come from? Why they're here?"

"I know why they're here," Big John said. "They're here to kill me."

"I'm sorry," Ray said. "About the smoke grenades." He knew his request would be the least popular with his own foxhole buddy.

Big John just shrugged. "Like the sergeant said, we ain't Marines 'cause it's easy." He grinned. "Shoulda nicknamed you 'Soft Spot.' Come on, Barbecue. Time to move out. Hopefully this dang rain will let up soon."

The squad gathered near Sergeant Meredith, and they were all about to move out when they heard a distinctive *pop*. Everyone froze. After several days on Okinawa, Ray knew exactly what that sound meant. They all did.

"Grenade!" Big John cried. "Hit the deck!"

But where? Who? Ray was about to throw himself into the mud when he caught Sergeant Meredith's wide, horror-filled eyes. Ray suddenly understood, and the bottom dropped out of his world.

One of the grenades in the sergeant's belt pouch had activated by accident, and it was going to explode in less than five seconds.

HIDEKI

SUTE-ISHI

"*Otō!*" Hideki cried.

As Hideki's eyes adjusted to the darkness inside his family tomb, he saw his father lying propped up against the stone caskets in the corner. Along the back wall of the tomb ran the shelves of urns that held the bones of his ancestors from generations past, including Shigetomo's.

A wide streak of blood trailed from the entrance of the tomb to Hideki's father, and Hideki's heart lurched.

"Otō, you're hurt!"

Hideki dropped the bag of the Emperor's photos by the door and ran to his father. Otō's breathing was ragged, and he slumped unnaturally to the side, one arm laid across his uniform jacket. Hideki lifted his father's hand away and saw a jagged wound in his stomach. His father had taken shrapnel from a grenade.

"A little run-in with the Americans," Otō said.

"We have to get you to a doctor!" Hideki cried.

"It's all right, Hideki. Someone is on the way," his father promised him. "But I could use some water."

Hideki grabbed an empty pot and ran through the rain to a nearby spring like it was the most important thing in the world. When he returned, he had to tip the pot to Otō's mouth for him. His father wasn't strong enough to hold it himself.

"You need the doctor," Hideki told his father. "I should go and find him."

Otō grabbed Hideki's arm with more strength than Hideki thought he had. "No. Don't go. I want you to clean the tomb while we wait."

"*Clean the tomb?*" Hideki said. "That doesn't matter right now."

"It always matters," Otō told him. He closed his eyes. "And make an offering. It's been too long."

Hideki didn't want to leave his father's side, but he did as he was told. The *haka* was dusty and full of cobwebs. In the past, they would never have let the family tomb become so untidy. But like their annual family picnic, the cleaning of the tomb had been set aside in their preparations for war. Failing to look after a *haka* brought sickness and death to a family, so cleaning it was doing *something* to help his father. At least that's what Hideki told himself. He found a broom and hastily swept the floor and shelves.

When he was finished, he took half the rice from the sock in Principal Kojima's bag and put it into a small stone bowl as an offering to Shigetomo and the rest of his ancestors. It wasn't as much as Hideki and his father usually left, but his ancestors had gone too long without any kind of offering, and it was as much as Hideki could spare.

"What's in the sack?" his father asked.

"Pictures of His Majesty the Emperor," Hideki said. "I'm keeping them safe."

His father closed his eyes again and shook his head. "No, Hideki. Forget about those things. You need to find your sister instead. She's all we have left."

"What do you mean?"

"Hideki, your mother and brother—they're dead."

Hideki's head spun. He couldn't believe what he was hearing. "But—no. No! They were evacuated to mainland Japan. They're safe."

His father shook his head. "Their ship was torpedoed by an American submarine," Otō said. "No one on board survived."

Hideki sat down on the cold floor of the family tomb. Shock washed over him like a wave. It couldn't be true. "No. I would have heard," Hideki said. "At school. They would have told us."

"The Japanese army forbade anyone to talk about it. It was bad for morale. But it's true, Hideki. I was at headquarters when the news came in. The ship was sunk the day after it left Naha Harbor. They stopped the evacuations after that."

Hideki reeled. He had almost been aboard that ship! If he hadn't decided to stay and fight, he'd be dead now too. His eyes fell on a cobweb he'd missed in his haste, and he felt sick to his stomach. Hideki had always resented having to clean the family tomb, but now he saw what disaster neglecting it could bring.

"I should never have sent them away," Otō said. "And I should never have let the IJA have you and your sister. You're both going to die with the Japanese."

Hideki saw again in his mind's eye the awful carnage of the Blood and Iron Student Corps' failed attack on the Americans. It was hard not to agree with his father.

But he and his classmates were just students. Boys. Surely, the Imperial Japanese Army would fare better than the Blood and Iron Student Corps had against the invaders.

"No," Hideki said. "We have to win!"

Otō shook his head again. "Hideki, the Japanese were never going to win this fight. They knew that from the start. The generals withdrew the very best soldiers from Okinawa long ago and sent them to Taiwan. They didn't want them to die here with the rest of us. We're just here to slow the Americans down while the army sets up their real defenses on the mainland. We're a *sute-ishi* in Go. A sacrificial pawn."

Go was an ancient game from China with black and white stones, where the object was to capture as much territory as possible. Sometimes you had to play a stone you knew was going to get taken, but you did it to make your opponent play a stone that would hurt them later. But the Okinawans weren't stones to be won or lost. They were real people! Hideki couldn't believe the Emperor would just throw their lives away like that.

"But . . . the *Yamato*!" Hideki argued. "They wouldn't send the biggest battleship in the Japanese fleet if they thought—"

"The *Yamato* was sunk by American planes three weeks before it was supposed to get here," his father said. "No one is coming to save us, Hideki. That's why you have to save yourself. And your sister."

Hideki's father coughed up blood. Where was that doctor? *No one is coming to save us, Hideki.* That's what his father had said. What if Otō had been lying about a doctor coming to help him?

"Otō—" Hideki began, but suddenly he heard someone coming through the entrance of the tomb. The doctor, at last!

But as the shadow emerged from the doorway, Hideki saw it wasn't a doctor after all. It was a soldier.

RAY

CRYING IN THE RAIN

"Grenade! Grenade! Get down!" Big John yelled.

Ray dropped flat to the ground. Sergeant Meredith took two running steps from everybody else, unhooked his grenade pouch, and chucked it away as hard as he could.

Ray had just enough time to scream *"Sergeant!"* before—*BOOM!*—the pouch exploded and the sergeant was thrown back against the outside of the tomb like a rag doll. Mud and bits of shrapnel peppered Ray's helmet, but he wasn't hurt.

Big John looked up from the muck. "What the hell just happened?"

"Sergeant Meredith!" Ray cried. He was up and on his feet and slipping toward the sergeant before anyone else. "It was one of his grenades!" Ray told the others.

"In his pouch! One of the pins must have got caught on something and worked its way out!"

Sergeant Meredith had tried to twist away from the blast, but one whole side of him was torn up. He was still alive though.

"Somebody get on the radio and call for a medic!" the Old Man said.

"No time!" Big John said. He pushed his heavy rifle into Ray's hands, and with one great heave Big John picked up Sergeant Meredith and threw him onto his shoulder. "He's not going to die here. Not like this!" Big John told them, and he took off for camp at a run.

Ray and the others ran with him. Sergeant Meredith hung over Big John's shoulder, his unconscious face turned to the side, facing Ray.

Sergeant Meredith was the one who'd taught him how to survive. Sergeant Meredith was the one who'd given him his nickname. Sergeant Meredith was the one who had listened when Ray had argued for the Okinawans. Sergeant Meredith was the one who had taught Ray how to grieve for the death of a soldier.

Ray just hoped he wasn't going to have to grieve for Sergeant Meredith.

Back at camp, the medics whisked Sergeant Meredith away. Ray and his squad waited on pins and needles for word on the sergeant's condition.

News of a death finally came that day, but it wasn't Sergeant Meredith. It was Franklin D. Roosevelt. The president of the United States had died of a stroke.

Ray sat down on his helmet, stunned. Roosevelt had been president of the United States since Ray was six years old. FDR had led America into war after the Japanese bombed Pearl Harbor in 1941. Less than a year ago, he'd been reelected to a fourth term, which had never happened before with any US president. Roosevelt was well liked and respected among the Marines. A lot of them around the camp were shaken up by the news, and Ray saw one or two of them crying. Ray felt more shocked than anything.

"It's Jap propaganda," Gonzalez said. "It has to be."

"No, it came in over the radio from the ships offshore," a captain told them. "It's real."

"Who's in charge now, Vice President Truman?" Gonzalez asked. "What do you think he'll be like?"

"Doesn't matter," Big John said sourly. "Losing the sergeant means more than losing some politician off in Washington. The president dying don't change a dang thing for any of us on Okinawa."

"We don't know the sergeant is dead yet," Ray argued.

"No, but you saw him. Even if he lives, he's not coming back. After all those battles he lived through. To go out like that . . ." Big John shook his head.

"Still doesn't mean we can't be sad about the president," the Old Man said, but Big John just shrugged.

"Grenade!" someone yelled, and suddenly a live grenade plopped into the muck at their feet. *What? How—?* Ray thought, but before he or anyone else could leap away or drop flat, the grenade went off with an ear-splitting *BANG!*

Ray jumped out of his skin, and some of the other guys screamed, but the grenade hadn't exploded. The top had blown off it, but its iron pineapple shell was still intact. Ray staggered back. He didn't understand what was going on.

One of the recent replacement troops, Private Wilbert Zimmer, guffawed nearby. "I thought I shook all the powder out, but I guess there was a little left in there after all!" he crowed. But he was the only one laughing.

The grenade had just been a prank? Ray felt like he'd almost had a heart attack. He put a hand on a tree to steady himself.

Big John bellowed with rage and charged Zimmer, tackling him hard. Big John battered the private with his big powerful fists until Ray and the Old Man and three others could finally pull him off.

Private Zimmer's face was purple and his eyes were

swelling shut. "I was only joking!" he blubbered. "Nobody got hurt!"

"Sergeant Meredith was nearly killed by a grenade today, you idiot!" Gonzalez told him.

"I didn't know," Zimmer said. "I didn't know."

Ray woke to relieve Big John on second watch late that night. The rain was still pouring down, like heaven was crying for President Roosevelt, and for everyone they'd lost so far in the war.

"Word came down while you were sleeping," Big John whispered to Ray. "The sergeant made it. He's got his Golden Ticket. What we all want—medical evacuation to a hospital in Hawaii."

Ray wasn't sure he wanted to get hit by a grenade like Sergeant Meredith, even if it did mean a ticket to Hawaii. But hearing the sergeant was going to live took a huge weight off Ray. His fitful sleep in the foxhole had been full of nightmares about exploding grenades.

Even though Sergeant Meredith wouldn't be coming back, Ray felt like the sergeant was still with him, in a way. Not his ghost—he wasn't dead—but his spirit, maybe. Like a part of the sergeant would always stay with him.

"Who's our new sergeant going to be?" Ray whispered.

"You're looking at him," Big John whispered back. Big John had been given a field promotion from Corporal to Sergeant. He was their squad leader now.

Big John settled back into the foxhole and closed his eyes. "Sergeant Meredith got out just in time. We've been ordered to the front first thing in the morning." He opened his eyes to look at Ray. "Everything we been through ain't nothing compared to what comes next."

HIDEKI

A BLESSING

A soldier stood silhouetted in the little door to Hideki's family tomb. It was too dark to see if he was Japanese or American, and Hideki fumbled for one of the grenades in his pocket. He'd just got hold of one when the soldier stepped farther into the tomb. It was a Japanese soldier! A private. Hideki could tell from the single star on his collar.

Otō put a hand on Hideki's arm, quietly signaling him to put away his grenade. "Welcome to the Kaneshiro family tomb, Private . . . ?"

"Shinohara," the private said. He scanned the room with the wild urgency of a trapped animal. His uniform was torn and covered in dirt and blood. Somewhere along the way he'd apparently lost his rifle, because all he carried was his sword.

Hideki stood at attention. A private was the lowest rank in the Japanese army, but privates still outranked every boy in the Blood and Iron Student Corps.

"Is there anybody else here?" the private demanded. "Have you seen any other soldiers, from either side?"

"No, sir," Hideki answered, careful to use Japanese. "Not since yesterday. But we're expecting a doctor soon."

Private Shinohara scoffed. "A doctor? Ha."

His eyes fell on the stone bowl with its tiny offering of food, and he pounced on it, scooping out the rice and stuffing it in his mouth.

"Hey! What are you doing? Stop!" Hideki said, forgetting the private's rank. "That's an offering! You can't eat that!"

Hideki's father reached out for him again. "Hideki, don't."

The private ignored them both and ate the rice. Hideki burned inside, but there was nothing he could do. Besides outranking Hideki, the private was bigger and stronger than he was. And the private had a sword.

When the private was finished gulping down the rice, he grabbed one of the large urns off a shelf and moved it near the door.

"What are you doing?" Hideki cried again. "This is my family's tomb! This is a sacred place!"

"It's an IJA base now," the private told him.

Hideki looked to his father for help, but Otō had his eyes closed and was slumped over to the side again. Where was that doctor?

Private Shinohara went to pull another urn from the shelf, and Hideki grabbed his arm and tried to yank him away. The private threw Hideki to the ground and pulled his sword from its scabbard with a *shing*. It glinted in the dim light from the entrance.

"Get out!" the private roared. "This is my hiding place. Get out! This cave is for army personnel only!"

"This tomb belongs to me and my family!" Hideki told him. "Besides, I'm in the army too! I'm in the Blood and Iron Student Corps!"

The private looked incredulous. "You're not in the real army. You're not even real Japanese! Get out!" The private took a swing at Hideki with his sword, and Hideki jumped back out of the way. Hideki's blood boiled. He was being attacked by someone from his own side, in his own family's tomb! He thought about going for a grenade again. But what was he going to do? Blow up a Japanese soldier? And himself and his father and his family tomb with him? But they couldn't stay here with Private Shinohara. The man was crazy.

Hideki got under his father's shoulder and lifted. Otō moaned in pain, but he stood, putting most of his weight on his son. Hideki steered them toward the door. Anger rose in Hideki like the tide. This was stupid!

They shouldn't have to be running from their own family's tomb. But Hideki didn't see that they had any other choice.

Private Shinohara kept his sword pointed at them the whole way, a mad gleam in his eyes. "Get out. Get out!" he roared. "If you *dojin* could defend your own stupid island, I wouldn't even be here!"

Hideki picked up the sack with the pictures of the Emperor, and he and his father staggered out into the rain. They made it as far as a nearby banyan tree before they both collapsed in a heap. Otō cried out again.

"I'm going to get you a doctor!" Hideki said. He stood up to go but Otō called him back.

"No, Hideki. Don't leave me."

"But you said someone was on the way."

"Yes. Death is on the way for me, Hideki," his father said. "There is no doctor coming. I came back to our family tomb to die."

Hideki's insides felt hollow. His father had been lying to him! Hideki had suspected it all along, but he hadn't wanted to believe it. And now it was too late.

Hideki dropped to his knees and sobbed. "No, Otō. No!"

"Don't cry, Hideki. This is a blessing."

"*A blessing?*" Hideki said.

"I got to see you again," his father said. It was harder and harder for him to breathe. "I never thought I'd see any of you again before . . ." Otō's eyes were a million miles away.

"You're going to be all right," Hideki told him. "I'm going to find a doctor. You're going to live."

But Hideki's words were empty, and they both knew it.

"I should have kept our family together," Otō muttered.

"There was nothing you could have done," Hideki told him. "There's nothing any of us could have done."

"You must find your sister," Otō said. He stopped to cough. "Forget this war and those stupid photographs. Find Kimiko and get yourselves to safety. That's all that matters now."

"You died a hero, Otō," Hideki said. "Fighting for Japan. I'll tell everyone."

His father laughed. It turned into another painful cough. "I'm no hero. I was so scared I pissed my pants. I was hit as I was running away."

Hideki was stunned. "But—but I'm the one who carries Shigetomo's curse, not you."

"Shigetomo wasn't a coward," Hideki's father said. "He was brave. Braver than any of us. I understand that now, and I hope one day you will too, before it's too late."

Shigetomo *brave*? Hideki couldn't believe what his father was saying.

Otō grabbed Hideki's jacket. His eyes were wide,

desperate and pleading. *"Find your sister.* Promise me you'll find her."

"I promise, Otō," Hideki said, frightened.

"Yes. Good." His father let go of him and slumped back against one of the roots hanging down from the branches of the banyan tree. "There are evil spirits all around, Hideki. More than ever. But evil can only run in a straight line. Keep changing course so the evil can't . . . can't catch . . ."

Otō's eyes still glistened, still stared up into the falling rain, but his chest stopped rising and falling. His body settled down into the mud.

Hideki's father was dead.

"No. *No!* Otō! Come back! Otō!" Hideki sobbed. He lay across his father's chest and cried as he hugged him good-bye.

Hideki couldn't carry his father back into the family tomb, not with Private Shinohara there. And he didn't have a shovel to bury him. He would have to leave him here, underneath this banyan tree, and come back later, after the war, and give his father a proper burial. Until then, Hideki would fulfill his father's dying wish and do the thing Otō had failed to do in life.

No matter where she was, no matter what she was doing, Hideki would find his sister.

RAY

MONSTER

Ray and his squad were a few hours into their rainy march when he heard explosions. He ducked instinctively, but the bombs weren't on top of them. Not yet.

"Japanese mortars," Big John said.

Things weren't going well on the front lines. So, as Big John had promised, the First Marines were being ordered south to fight there. The soldiers of the Army's 96th Division currently fighting at the front were to swap places with them, continuing the lighter duty of clearing caves and securing the northern part of the island while they recuperated.

"How can you tell one explosion from another?" Ray asked.

"You get shot at enough times, you get to recognizing the sound," Big John told him.

"You haven't faced mortars yet, have you Barbecue?" the Old Man asked, walking alongside them. "Mortars lob bombs at you from a long way off. Like a long fly ball." The Old Man whistled while he made an arcing motion with his hand. "Lot of new guys, they don't know the secret to running through mortar fire."

"Run zigzag?" Ray guessed.

The Old Man shook his head. "No. You run straight away. No turning, no looking back. That's how you survive a mortar attack."

Stay low, don't bunch up, and run like hell, Ray thought. Just what the sergeant had told him as they came off the boat. Sergeant Meredith, that was. Ray had to remember that Big John was their sergeant now.

Stark's long legs took him on ahead, and Big John fell in beside Ray as they walked.

"I love the Old Man like a brother," Big John said, "but he's dead wrong about how to survive a mortar attack, Barbecue."

Ray frowned. "I should run zigzag after all?"

"Naw. The secret to running through artillery is that it doesn't matter what you do," he told Ray. "You zig, you may make it. You zag, you may get hit. There's a bomb or a bullet or a grenade out there with everybody's name on it, and if it's gonna get you it's gonna get you."

That was a hell of a way to live your life, Ray

thought. Knowing that death could catch up to you any second and that nothing you did made a difference. Ray wondered again about his father in the First World War. Hiding in foxholes, pinned down by Germans, listening to the bombs explode all around him. Had he also expected death any second? Was that what had broken him? Made him into a monster?

Ray touched the long scar on the inside of his left arm and remembered how he'd gotten it. Ray had been shooting a rifle since he was six, and every winter it was his job to shoot the hogs before he and his father hung them up to butcher them. It had been the same every year, until he was eleven years old. That year, Ray's father had stood to the side with his butcher knife like always, waiting for Ray to put down one of the pigs. But that year, everything went wrong.

Usually, one .22 rifle slug was enough to kill a pig. But this pig didn't die with one shot. It took the bullet and squealed, staggering away. The high-pitched screeching was the most awful thing Ray had ever heard, and he immediately felt sick. He hadn't meant for the pig to suffer. Ray hurried to take aim with his rifle again, to put the poor thing out of its misery.

And that's when his father had gone crazy.

"*No!*" Ray's father screamed. "Stay away from him! Get away!" And suddenly he ran at Ray with the butcher knife. Ray got the rifle up just in time to block the first of his father's slashes, but the next one caught Ray on the inside of his left arm, carving a deep gash from his wrist almost all the way down to his elbow. Ray screamed and dropped the rifle. He ducked his father's next attack and ran for the house, clutching his arm to his chest. His mother drove him to the hospital for stitches, and when they got back, his father wouldn't look him in the eye. But Pa had never apologized, never tried to explain, and none of them had spoken a word about what happened ever again.

As many times as Ray had replayed that day in his head, he had still never understood exactly what it was that had set his father off. Was it the gunshot? The pig's squealing? Ray chasing it down? Like all the other times his father had gotten violent and unpredictable, there was no understandable reason for it. But that time had been the worst. That time it had cost Ray two pints of blood and the last bit of love he'd had for his father.

"Okinawans!" somebody yelled, waking Ray from his reverie. "Refugees coming through the lines!"

Ray instinctively tightened his grip on his rifle, and he saw the other Marines raise theirs under their rain capes. Big John had kept Sergeant Meredith's new rule about not killing Okinawans. But any encounter made the squad jumpy.

There was no mistaking these people as anything but refugees though. Their hair and clothes were filthy, they had scratches and poorly bandaged wounds, and none of them looked like they'd had a good meal in a month. But the worst part was the fear on their faces, like Ray and all the others were the most frightening monsters they'd ever seen. Some of them couldn't even look at the Marines, they were so scared.

If they're so frightened of us, what are they doing here? Ray wondered. He lowered his rifle and started for a woman with a baby in her arms.

"Some of 'em are Jap soldiers!" Big John cried.

Ray watched in stunned horror as a Japanese soldier dressed as one of the Okinawans tossed aside the ratty blanket he hid beneath and shot the Old Man dead. More Japanese soldiers did the same, and all hell broke loose.

"Don't let 'em through! Shoot! Shoot!" Big John yelled, and the Marines opened up on them. They didn't know who was Japanese and who was Okinawan, and they didn't wait to find out.

When the last rifle fired, the Marines stood in the pouring rain surrounded by bodies. Some of the dead were American Marines. Some were Japanese soldiers. But many more of them were Okinawans. Refugees who had needed their help.

Ray let the tip of his rifle drop into the mud and looked around in horror. In his panic he'd fired round after round into the crowd. He had to have killed innocent Okinawans. He knew it. In just a few awful seconds, he had become the monster these people were so afraid of. More of a monster than his father had ever been.

And the worst part was, Ray knew he would do it again when he had to.

HIDEKI

THE HOLE IN THE WALL

Hideki didn't know where his sister was now, but he knew the last place she'd been before the American monsters came: her high school. That was where he decided to start.

The schoolhouse was still standing when he got there, but a big hole had been blown in one side of it by an American bomb.

"Kimiko!" Hideki cried. He dropped the sack with the Emperor's photographs and ran inside.

What he saw made him gasp.

Students lay dead all around Hideki. Some of them had been thrown across the room by the blast. Others were slumped over their desks. The bomb had hit while the students were in class.

Hideki would have retched if he'd had anything in his stomach.

He wanted to run, to get as far away from this horrible scene as he could, but Hideki had to know if any of the girls was his sister. He went up and down the rows of desks, examining each girl's face. But none of them was Kimiko. He was sure of it. Relief washed over him. It felt wrong to be happy his sister wasn't here when so many other girls hadn't been so lucky, but it meant there was a chance his sister was still alive somewhere.

Kimiko had been one of the older girls at the school. Perhaps she had already been sent to her nursing assignment. But where?

Hideki searched the room for clues. There were still lessons scratched on the board, the neat *kanji* starting in the upper right corner and moving down and left across the blackboard. A Japanese language lesson. On the wall beside the blackboard, next to the hole the bomb had made, was a framed photo of the school's faculty and students. The girls wore their best clothes—kimonos for some, fancy Western dresses for others—and their male teachers wore kimonos or jackets and ties.

There was a brighter spot on the wall next to the photograph where another frame had hung but was now missing. A picture of His Majesty the Emperor, Hideki guessed. Someone had taken it, no doubt to try to protect the Emperor's *mabui*, but they had left the photo of the girls where it was.

Hideki examined the papers scattered around the room. Most of them were pages of student work, but one was an official communication from army headquarters. It ordered all fifth-year girls from the school to report to the army hospital in Ichinichibashi. Hideki's heart leaped. Kimiko was a fifth-year student! That must be where she was! But Ichinichibashi was a town on the southern part of the island. The same direction the American monsters were going.

Hideki would have to get past them to find his sister.

I can't do it, he thought. He remembered the disastrous first meeting of the Americans and the Blood and Iron Student Corps, and he was frightened all over again. It would be so much easier to run north, to hide in the part of the island the Americans had already passed through. But it was his father's dying wish that Hideki find Kimiko, to restore what was left of their family. And Hideki had promised him he would.

The hole in the wall of the school was like the lens of a camera, and through it Hideki saw Shuri Castle in the distance. Shuri Castle was a big four-story red building—the biggest in all of Okinawa—with a Chinese pagoda-style roof and ornate columns.

Hideki thought of what Lieutenant Tanaka, the

photographer, had said. What story did this picture tell? What had happened before this moment? What was happening now? What would happen next?

What had come before, Hideki had learned in school: For hundreds of years, Shuri Castle had been the royal palace of the Ryukyu Kingdom. Then the Japanese had invaded and conquered Okinawa in 1609—that fateful year Shigetomo had cursed his clan forever with his cowardice.

Now? Now the Japanese army ruled the island from the caves and tunnels Hideki and his classmates had helped dig beneath Shuri Castle last year. The castle was a fortress, and so was Okinawa. That was the story Hideki saw, and it gave him hope that the Imperial Japanese Army would win and he might actually find his sister.

What happened next? Hideki would step into the picture. Head south, toward Ichinichibashi and Kimiko. Shuri Castle was on the way, and if there was anyplace safe on the whole island, IJA headquarters had to be it.

Hideki heard strange voices outside, and he froze. American soldiers! A whole platoon of them, coming into the village! His hand went to one of the grenades in his pocket, but just as quickly he let it go. He might be able to kill one or two soldiers, but the others would kill Hideki just as quick, and then he would never find his sister. He had to find somewhere to hide instead.

Hideki heard a creak on the porch steps and threw himself onto one of the empty desks. He flopped over the desktop and pretended to be dead. It wasn't hard. His uniform shirt and pants were so filthy they were unrecognizable, and his hair was matted and mangy. A buzzing fly crawled over his hands and face and up inside his cap.

His cap! Hideki whipped it off his head and dropped it at his feet. He flopped back down on the desktop just seconds before the American soldier came in the room. Would the American see his cap? Would Hideki have to kill him with his grenade after all?

Hideki kept his eyes screwed shut and held his breath, his heart pounding in his chest. Heavy boots shuffled a few steps into the room and then stopped. Had the soldier spotted him? Was he aiming his rifle at Hideki right now? Hideki waited, his lungs burning, sweat soaking his back. When Hideki didn't hear anything more for almost a full minute, he pried his eyes open to take a peek.

There he was. An American soldier. Not much older than he was, Hideki realized with a start. He didn't even have a beard. His face was round and freckled. He wore a big green-and-brown poncho over his backpack and a matching helmet on his head, both of which made him look more like a turtle-man than a soldier. He was wet and mucky, just like Hideki, and he dripped water on the dry floor.

The soldier hadn't spotted Hideki. He was looking instead at the framed picture of the students and faculty. What in the world did he want with that?

The soldier stared at it for a few seconds more, then took the photograph out of its frame. The soldier folded the picture in half and put it in a pocket under his poncho.

But why? Hideki wondered. Did the soldier know one of the girls in the photograph? Was he tracking one of them down? Was there something special about this school?

"Rei?" a man called from outside. He asked a question in English that Hideki didn't understand, and then called the soldier's name again. "Rei?"

The soldier in the room with Hideki called back, and Hideki squeezed his eyes shut and played dead as the soldier picked up his rifle and left. Hideki didn't breathe again until the soldier was long gone.

RAY

DECEASED

Ray looked at the picture he'd taken from the school-room as he and his platoon continued their march south. The strangest thing about the photo was that no one was smiling. It was like they all knew they were going to end up dead in that classroom. Ray wondered if the sailors on the battleships would still have fired if they knew they were killing schoolchildren. Whole villages of innocent people.

But *he* had done that. So why should the sailors be any different?

Big John put an arm around Ray's neck and gave him a playful headlock. "Still a softy after all this time, huh, Barbecue?"

Ray tried to smile. Big John liked to talk tough, and he *was* tough, but Big John did have a heart inside that big barrel chest of his. Ray was sure of it. It had just been hardened over by combat. Ray had learned to hate the Japanese as much as Big John and the other old-timers did, but he still held out hope Big John would start to see the Okinawans differently.

The big guns of the US Navy fleet offshore erupted like thunder, and Ray and Big John froze. The battleships kept up a constant bombardment on the southern part of the island all day, and like the rain, everybody had just gotten used to it by now. But this was something new.

"It's different this time," Ray said. He was surprised to find he'd been around long enough to realize it. "I hear 16-inch, 5-inch, antiaircraft rockets. They're shooting everything at once."

Big John nodded.

"What is it? What's happening?" Zimmer asked.

"Has to be a Jap counterattack. Big one," Big John said.

They all waited while Gonzalez radioed in. He blinked in surprise when he finally got through and learned what it was.

"They're celebrating," he told them. "Germany surrendered. Hitler committed suicide. The Nazis are through."

Ray felt himself go slack. He knew he should be happy about the news—the war in Europe had been going on for six long years, and it had cost the lives of millions of people, soldiers and civilians alike. And he *was* glad it was over, for the sake of all the people who were still fighting it. But it didn't change anything for Ray or his squad. Looking around at the rest of the Marines, he could see that most of them felt the same way.

"But . . . but that's great, isn't it?" Zimmer asked, seeing all the gloomy faces around him. He hadn't been on Okinawa long enough to understand.

"It's good and all," Big John said, "but Nazi Germany might as well be on the moon for all it matters to us."

Another sergeant brought a sack of mail up through the lines, and everyone gathered around to see if they had gotten a letter from home.

Ray had a letter from his mother. It was mostly about planting the new corn crop back on the farm in Nebraska, and what his young cousins were up to. But she had included a photograph too. It was a picture of Ray and his father at the state fair, mugging for the camera in silly pirate costumes. Ray had an eye patch and a fake beard and an old-fashioned flintlock pistol, and Pa wore a bandanna and brandished a wooden cutlass. They were laughing and leaning into each other, a loving father and son. Ray figured his mother had sent him the picture to remind him that his father wasn't always a terrible person, and for a moment it worked. Ray smiled to himself at the memory of that day, and he got homesick all over again.

But then Ray remembered a night not long after the one at the fair, when his Pa had stormed drunk from the house, leaving broken furniture in his wake. Ma had begged Ray not to judge his father too harshly. "He's not the man I married," she told Ray. "He was different before the war."

They were both different now—Ray and his father. But they were still the happy people in the photograph too, weren't they?

Could they be both at once?

"What'd you get, Busko?" Gonzalez asked one of the other Marines.

"Letter from my sweetheart, Sarah." Busko beamed. "She's training to be a teacher back in North Carolina. Met her on Atlantic Beach when I was down there training at Camp Lejeune."

"Gonna move in with her parents when you get back?" Zimmer kidded him.

"I hope not—her daddy runs a funeral home!"

"Hey, get this," Zimmer said. He held up a piece of paper. "I got a letter from the Missouri Department of Transportation. They say if I don't pay off my traffic tickets, they're gonna come arrest me!"

That got a lot of laughs. "Now, that I'd like to see!" Ray said.

"You oughtta let 'em do it," said Big John. "Even jail'd be better than this everlovin' rain."

As they got closer to the front lines, they passed exhausted soldiers headed north for a break. They were bloody and bandaged and muddy. They stumbled along, dog-tired, their heads down and eyes on the ground. On the rare occasion that one of them looked up, Ray saw that thousand-yard stare. They looked like ghosts. Ray felt a lead weight grow heavier in his stomach, and it got harder and harder to pick up his feet and move forward.

One of the ghosts glanced at Ray for a second as they passed. "Take plenty of grenades with you down there, Marine," he said.

Farther on, Ray saw the evidence of the hard-fought battle alongside the muddy road: empty ammo boxes, spent rifle clips, bloody bandages, bullet-riddled jackets and trousers. The American dead had already been removed, but there were dead Japanese everywhere.

Ray winced and had to look away. Ray was a hunter. He had killed deer and stripped their skins. But this was different. It was unnatural. Brutal. After seeing these horrible, broken bodies, Ray wasn't sure he could ever hunt again.

Just like Pa, Ray realized. It had always been Ray's uncle who took him hunting.

A sudden thought struck Ray: Was this why his Pa

had argued so strongly against him enlisting? Had his father actually been trying to *protect* Ray from becoming the monster he had become?

Mortar shells exploded along the road, and Ray and his squad dove facedown into the muck. Mud and rock geysered up around them, and the earth shook with the thunder of artillery. The Japanese were shooting at them in the daylight? This never happened up north!

"Into the foxholes!" Big John bellowed, and they leaped into trenches that had been dug and re-dug a dozen times since Love Day a month ago. Ray held on to his helmet while the mortars fell all around them with the rain.

"Zimmer! Lemme see that letter you got from the Missouri D.O.T.!" Big John hollered.

Zimmer didn't understand and neither did anyone else, but he handed it over anyway. Big John took a grease pencil out of his pocket and scrawled the word DECEASED across the envelope in big block letters.

"There you go," Big John said. "Now you can send that back to them in advance, and they won't bother you no more."

HIDEKI

YŌKAI

Hideki's foot stuck in the mud. He tugged and tugged on it until his foot came right out of his boot. It took him ages to dig his boot out in the darkness.

When he could finally walk again, Hideki staggered to the top of a hill and stopped for a minute, bone-weary. He had to travel by night—that was the only time the American battleships stopped shelling the island.

Hideki made sure he was still pointed toward the dark silhouette of Shuri Castle in the distance. If Shuri Castle was still standing, the Americans couldn't be winning too much. Hideki felt a swell of pride at that. As long as Shuri Castle still stood, so too did Okinawa.

Hideki took another step forward and his feet went out from under him. He fell on his back, and suddenly he was tumbling and sliding down a steep, muddy slope. He crashed into the shattered remains of tree stumps but bounced off them, was lashed by saplings but couldn't grab them. There was nothing he could do to stop his long, dizzying barrel roll down the hill until he plunged headfirst into a pool of mud.

Hideki's skin crawled, and with a horrified yelp, he realized he was covered in maggots. They were in his hair and inside his shirt and down his pants. Hideki screamed and scrambled away, tearing at his clothes. He stripped off his shirt and his shoes and his pants and both socks—even the shorts he wore as underpants.

Hideki ran his shaking hands over every inch of his body, now glad for the pounding, incessant rain that washed him clean. His skin still crawled, and his shuddering turned into a constant tremble in the cold rain. Hideki wrapped his arms around himself and shivered. But he would not put his clothes back on. Not with them covered in maggots.

Hideki had never felt so naked before. So utterly helpless and exposed. Everything he was, the person he had been, all of it had been stripped away. He was nothing. Nobody.

He was a ghost.

Hideki's ceramic grenades glistened in the mud. Miraculously, they hadn't cracked in the fall. Hideki remembered Lieutenant Colonel Sano's words to him and all the other boys: *One grenade is for the American monsters coming to kill your family. You are to use the other grenade to kill yourself.* Hideki hadn't used either of his grenades. He'd been too frightened to throw one at the Americans. Might be too frightened to *ever* throw one at the Americans.

Did that mean he should use one on himself here and now? The way Lieutenant Colonel Sano had told him?

Hideki wanted to. No—that wasn't true. He didn't want to be *here*, now. He didn't want to be naked and shivering and afraid. But he didn't want to die. And if he used his grenade on himself, he could never fulfill his promise to his father to find his sister.

Still shivering, Hideki picked up the sack with the photos of His Majesty the Emperor. Some pictures had fallen out and he had no hope of finding them, but he saved what he could.

The sack and his two grenades were all he took with him.

Hideki trudged on until he heard voices in the darkness—foreign voices, Americans. *Will they even see me?* Hideki wondered. *Am I really a ghost?*

But no, he must be alive. Not even death could be this cold. Hideki gave the American camp a wide berth, his eyes searching the darkness for anything that might give him shelter or warmth.

There—a blacker spot in the darkness. Was that the

opening of a cave? So close to the American camp? Hideki staggered over to it.

"*Yōkai,*" someone whispered at him out of the darkness.

Hideki froze. *Yōkai* was the Japanese word for a spirit. A ghost.

"I—I'm not a *yōkai,*" Hideki said, his teeth chattering. "I'm—"

"*What is the password?*" the voice said.

Hideki suddenly understood. The man was a Japanese soldier, and *yokai* was the challenge word of the day. If Hideki wanted to come through, he had to know the response.

"*Yuta?*" Hideki guessed.

Suddenly, a Japanese guard stuck a rifle in his face.

Hideki had guessed wrong.

The soldier snatched Hideki's grenades and led him into the cave at gunpoint. A covered light helped Hideki's eyes adjust, and he saw the floor of the main cavern was filled with wounded Japanese soldiers. More IJA soldiers with rifles squatted here and there, and at the back of the cave, huddled together, were ten Okinawans, mostly women and children.

"Who's this?" an IJA lieutenant demanded.

"An Okinawan boy! I caught him outside," said Hideki's captor. "He didn't know the password. He had these grenades on him. I think he's a spy!"

"I'm not a spy!" Hideki cried. "My name is Hideki Kaneshiro! I'm a member of the Blood and Iron Student Corps. And look—" He opened the sack of photos he carried. "I've been protecting images of His Majesty the Emperor!"

The lieutenant nodded his approval. "All right. Get a new uniform over there."

The corner the lieutenant pointed to was stacked with the bodies of dead Japanese soldiers. He meant for Hideki to take the clothes off a dead man.

Hideki did as he was told. He found a jacket and pants that fit him if he rolled up the cuffs. The pants had bullet holes in them, but at least they were warm. He found a helmet too, but none of the dead soldiers had shoes small enough for Hideki's feet. He went barefoot instead.

"Water. Bring us water," one of the injured soldiers moaned. Another grabbed at Hideki's trouser legs.

"Get over here!" the lieutenant barked at Hideki. "We're planning an attack."

An attack? On who, the Americans? But that was crazy! There were only seven healthy soldiers, including the lieutenant.

"The wounded men need water," Hideki told the lieutenant.

"Don't waste your time on them," the lieutenant said. "They'll be dead soon anyway. The time has come for a counterattack. There is an American camp nearby.

We will leave the cave and surprise them just before dawn."

Hideki couldn't believe what he was hearing. "But the Americans have lots more men than we do," he told the officers. "They'll kill us all!"

The lieutenant ignored him. "Issue grenades to the wounded soldiers who can't march and tell them to kill themselves when we're gone. They are not to be captured by the enemy. Any soldier who can walk comes with us on the attack."

"That's still not enough!" Hideki argued.

"Be quiet!" the lieutenant cried. He struck Hideki across the face with the back of his hand, sending Hideki to the floor. "Junior officers will speak only when spoken to!" The lieutenant turned to one of his men. "Get the Okinawans," he said. "We'll strap explosives to them and send them out ahead of us."

Hideki watched, aghast, as two of the soldiers dragged an Okinawan woman and her baby out of the corner. The woman was wearing a beautiful blue *bashōfu* kimono with white flowers on it. How she had managed to keep it clean so long while a battle was raging all around them, Hideki had no idea.

Hideki blinked. Suddenly, he saw the woman as though she and her kimino had been tinted by a photographer—the only spot of color painted on a black-and-white photograph of the war.

And then the soldiers tied a belt of dynamite around her waist.

Hideki lurched forward, trying to stop them. "No! You can't! They're not soldiers!"

The lieutenant shoved Hideki back and pulled out his pistol. "You will fight! You will *all* fight! This is *your* island, after all!" the lieutenant spat. Hideki was still reeling as the lieutenant slapped the ceramic grenades back into Hideki's hands. "You should all be the ones dying to defend it, not us!"

This was crazy. Hideki slipped the grenades into his jacket pockets and staggered back, looking for someplace to run, someplace to hide. But there was no other exit from the cave.

The lieutenant pointed his pistol at them all, Okinawans and Japanese alike.

"Now—attack!" the lieutenant screamed. "For Japan! For the Emperor! *Attack!*"

RAY

KAKAZU RIDGE

"All right, boys, let's show 'em what the Marines can do!" Big John yelled. *"Attack!"*

Ray took a deep breath and climbed over the ledge of their foxhole. *Stay low, don't bunch up, and run like hell*, he reminded himself.

The running like hell was the easy part—Ray was so scared he ran like a locomotive was bearing down on him. Big John did the same on one side of him, Gonzalez on the other.

The hill above them was called Kakazu Ridge. For more than a month, the army had tried to take this one little hill from the Japanese, and every single time the Japanese had beaten them back.

Now it was the Marines' turn.

Ray, Big John, and Gonzalez stayed five paces apart

and ran low as bullets began to *fwip* into the mud at their feet. A mortar blew up to the left of Ray, and just like that Gonzalez was gone. *Gonzalez!*

Ray couldn't stop. Couldn't think about it. He kept running uphill, his heart thumping so hard he thought it would burst. He slipped and slid as he tried to get traction up the slope, hauling himself up on shredded tree stumps and saplings when he could. Bullets zipped. Grenades boomed. And then suddenly Ray was at the top of the ridge. What they called the "saddle"—the gap in the ridge where two hills came together. Ray could see a small valley just beyond Kakazu, and another, taller mountain range on the other side. The valley might once have been green and lush, but the naval bombardment had left it a stumpy, blackened wasteland filled with giant craters. It was like looking down on the moon.

Ray didn't have much more time to take in the scenery. He dropped flat and dragged Zimmer down beside him. Somehow the rookie had survived the charge. Big John had too. He flopped down next to Ray in the saddle as blue tracer fire from a Japanese machine gun skimmed the air right above them. A fourth Marine, a recruit so new Ray didn't even know his name, collapsed on the other side of Big John.

"Am I dead?" Zimmer asked. "Am I a ghost?"

"You're not dead," Ray said. "Not yet. But what do

we do now, Sergeant?" Nobody else had made the saddle with them.

Big John didn't seem to hear him, and that's when Ray noticed he wasn't wearing his helmet anymore. He didn't have a right ear anymore, either.

"Big John! Your ear!" Ray yelled. It was a bloody mess, but Big John didn't seem to notice until Ray pointed to it. Ray dug in his web pack for bandages and wrapped Big John's head for him.

"Huh," Big John said, peering over the side of the ridge while Ray worked on him. "I think I can see my house from here."

"I can't see a blessed thing!" Zimmer said. He had his face in the mud and his arms around his head.

They were mercifully safe here in the gap between the ridges. But the rest of the battalion was taking heavy fire trying to get all the way to the tops of Kakazu and Kakazu West.

"What do we do?" Ray asked again, this time yelling loud enough that Big John could hear him.

Big John lay on his back, hugging his big BAR like a security blanket. "I figure if we lay low here long enough, some of those Japs from the south slope are going to get it in their heads they can counterattack. That means they gotta come right through us. Turn around and get yourselves in position."

Ray was already in position. But aiming at any

attacking soldiers meant raising his head, and it sounded like the bullets were missing him by inches. It took every ounce of courage he had just to shift his face to the side, and he held his breath as he twisted his chin forward.

Come on, Ray, he told himself. *You're not gonna die with your eyes closed.*

Ray let out his breath and opened his eyes. It wasn't much of a view—just more mud and coral and the little lip at the edge of the saddle that had kept them all from dying for the past five minutes. Beyond that, through the haze of smoke from mortar and artillery fire, Ray could see a sliver of the green mountains beyond. That was where the Japanese soldiers would come from, if they came at all.

No sooner had Ray thought it than the mortars and grenades stopped falling. He tightened his grip on his rifle. If the IJA wasn't shooting anymore, that could only mean one thing: The Japanese were about to storm Kakazu Ridge themselves.

HIDEKI

RUN

***"Banzai!"* the Japanese lieutenant yelled as the soldiers** and refugees streamed outside.

Hideki didn't want to die. Shigetomo's *mabui* took over, and Hideki ducked the lieutenant's bamboo stick and fled deeper into the cave.

"You! Get back here, you coward!" the lieutenant cried. He raised his pistol and pulled the trigger.

PAKOW! The sound of the lieutenant's gun was so loud in the little cave that Hideki was sure he'd been shot. He flinched and stumbled to the ground, scuffing his knees. But he wasn't shot. The bullet had missed him. Heart pounding, Hideki scrambled to his feet and snatched up the sack with the Emperor's photos. But there was nowhere to run. The front entrance was the only way in or out of the cave. Hideki's breath came hard and quick as he backed away.

The lieutenant's eyes were wide with madness. He aimed the gun at Hideki again.

Pakow. Hideki's eardrums were so damaged that the sound was muted now, but he felt the sting of the bullet as it grazed his arm. It burned white hot, like touching a pot that had been too long over the fire. He cried out, his own voice muffled to him.

The sound of the gunshots had hurt the lieutenant's hearing too. He winced, closing his eyes and holding his ears. In moments, Hideki knew, the lieutenant would recover and take another shot. Hideki searched desperately for some way to escape.

The air shafts! These man-made caves had air vents cut into them, leading up to the surface.

While the lieutenant still had his eyes closed, Hideki slipped the string of the sack of photos around his neck and scrambled up a hill of dead bodies and into the air shaft above them. There weren't many places to hang on, but he managed to wedge his knees against the hard rock to hold himself in place. The sack weighed him down and he struggled to climb, his knees barking in pain, his arm burning and bleeding.

Hideki looked down, worried that the lieutenant was going to appear underneath him any moment. But the lieutenant must not have seen him climb into the air shaft. He cried out in surprise, demanding Hideki come out from wherever he was hiding.

That gave Hideki a panicky few seconds to claw himself higher, higher. Just as his hand found the wooden frame at the top of the shaft, he heard the lieutenant cry out again. He'd spotted Hideki! He was looking right up the air shaft!

The lieutenant yelled something at him, something Hideki's ringing ears couldn't understand, and Hideki heaved himself up and out of the air shaft as another bullet from below hit the wooden frame, showering him with splinters.

But he was free.

Hideki crawled out onto a hilltop studded with broken tree stumps. There was no chance the tall lieutenant could follow him up the shaft—Hideki himself had barely fit. And the entrance to the cave was nowhere nearby. He was safe. For now.

His limbs near useless, ears still pounding, Hideki rolled into one of the water-filled craters that pitted the ground.

As he lay half submerged, he began to cry again. Great wracking sobs he couldn't control. Hideki cried for the Okinawans he'd watched get strapped with explosives. He cried for the Japanese soldiers who lay dying in the cave. He cried out of sheer exhaustion. He even cried for the awful lieutenant. Hideki cried until he had no more tears to shed, and then the Okinawan sky cried for him, raining down its own cold tears.

His father was right. Okinawa was a *sute-ishi.* A sacrificial stone. Just like the Blood and Iron Student Corps. The Japanese army had sent him and the other boys out to fight against an experienced, well-equipped American killing machine with nothing more than a few days' training and two grenades each. They *expected* them to die. The Japanese army didn't care about "protecting" Okinawa or its people. All they cared about was buying themselves enough time to defend their *own* islands.

Hideki's face burned hot with anger and shame. He'd believed everything they'd told him. Swallowed all their insults and lies. And for what?

Hideki picked up the sack with the images of His Majesty the Emperor of Japan and flung it away with a scream, picture frames spilling out into the mud. Hideki was done. Finished. There was nothing left to fight for, and certainly nothing left to die for. He would find a squad of American soldiers and surrender to them, just like the leaflets had told him to.

Hideki trudged down the other side of the hill, slipping and sliding in the muck. He spotted American soldiers up ahead, clearing a cave.

Hideki froze, watching in horror as the Americans fired a flamethrower through the cave's tiny entrance.

They hadn't even checked to see if it was soldiers or civilians inside!

One American soldier spotted Hideki and pointed. He yelled something.

Suddenly, the other soldiers turned and aimed their guns right at him.

"No—wait!" Hideki cried.

Another American with a huge gas tank on his back turned on Hideki with wild eyes—blazing, crazy eyes like the ones Hideki had seen on the lieutenant in the cave. Liquid flame spurted out from the nozzle of the American's flamethrower. *Fwoosh!*

Hideki was far enough away that the flames just brushed him, singeing his eyebrows and setting the front of his uniform on fire. He stumbled backward into the mud, desperately patting out the flames. Bullets buzzed like mosquitoes in his ears, and he turned and ran. They were *all* monsters, the Japanese *and* the Americans, and he zigged and he zagged, trying to escape their evil spirits, just like his father had taught him.

Hideki didn't know where he was, or where he was going. He just knew he never wanted to see another American soldier again as long as he lived.

RAY

RUN

The Japanese were coming.

"Me and Barbecue'll take the first wave!" Big John yelled. "New guy, Zimmer, you're the second team. You fire while the first team reloads! Got it? Don't shoot 'til you see the whites of their eyes!"

Ray took aim through the sights on his rifle. At first he was just looking at green mountains and blue sky, and then suddenly there was a dirty green helmet, and then the face of a Japanese soldier, his eyes wide with surprise at seeing Ray and his rifle team. Ray raised himself up on his elbows and fired his M-1.

Pa-kow! The soldier fell backward down the slope. There was no time to think, no time to do anything but shoot again, and again, as Japanese soldier after

Japanese soldier tried to get high enough on the ridge to shoot them back.

"I'm almost out!" Ray yelled. *Click!* His clip was spent, but there was already another soldier in his sights. *Pa-kow!* Ray flinched as Zimmer took him down.

"Reload! Reload!" Big John yelled at him. Ray ejected his rifle's spent clip and scrambled for a new one from the pouches on his belt. He had another loaded and ready to go just in time for him and Big John to take over for Zimmer and the new guy when they ran out.

The Japanese kept coming, and Ray kept shooting. He had to. *Pakow. Pakow. Pakow.* How long had they been at this? It felt like hours, but Ray knew it had to only be minutes. His arms and shoulders ached.

"I'm running low on ammo!" the new guy yelled. Ray was low too. They all had to be. They didn't have an unlimited supply of bullets and grenades.

And then, as quickly as it had begun, it was over. The Japanese soldiers stopped coming, and Ray breathed a huge sigh of relief and checked his watch.

The whole counterattack had lasted no more than fifteen minutes.

"Hey. You guys still alive?" Big John asked.

"Just barely," Zimmer called back. The new guy was alive too.

Everything was still and quiet. The American mortars

weren't firing because they didn't want to hit any Marines left alive on the ridge, and for some reason the Japanese mortars hadn't started up again. The silence was almost more frightening than the attack. Ray knew some Japanese soldier was out there right now with his rifle trained on the very place he was hiding, just waiting for Ray to peek out.

"Now what do we do?" Ray asked.

"Hang on—somebody's coming!" Big John told them.

Another ground attack? Ray checked his ammunition. He only had two clips left. That was just sixteen bullets. They weren't going to be able to hold out much longer.

"Same pairs as before," Big John said, his voice hard. "When we're out, we're out, and we make a run for it."

The top of a head rose on the Japanese side of the saddle, and Ray took careful aim with his rifle. His finger tightened on the trigger as he waited for the soldier's eyes.

But it wasn't a soldier. It was an Okinawan woman! And there were more of them. Women. Children. Old men. *Refugees.* Dozens of them coming up the hill toward the saddle between the ridges. But why here? Why now?

The woman closest to Ray had on the most beautiful blue dress Ray had ever seen. It was covered with white flowers, white like fluffy clouds on a sunny summer day in Nebraska. Ray froze, the woman floating in front of him like some kind of vision. Who was she?

What was she doing here, in the middle of a firefight? How in the world had she kept that blue dress so clean when everything else was covered in mud?

The woman was sobbing, Ray noticed, and she held a baby in her arms. With sudden horror, Ray understood why these people were here, now, in the middle of a battlefield.

The woman had dynamite strapped around her waist.

The Japanese were using the Okinawans as human bombs.

"Shoot! Shoot them before they get too close!" Big John roared. Zimmer and the new guy fired, their fear overcoming their discipline.

But Ray was frozen. He couldn't do it. The woman in the beautiful blue dress staggered closer, closer, her arms wrapped tight around her baby. Protecting him from the monsters in their world.

"Barbecue! *Barbecue!*" Big John yelled, trying to snap him out of it. But Ray could already feel his rifle lowering. He couldn't shoot this woman. Wouldn't.

So Big John did it for him.

KABOOM!

Ray's skin glowed hot from the blast. He felt fuzzy-headed, dazed, like he did when he had the flu. He tried to shake it off, to come back to his senses.

"My rifle's overheating!" Zimmer cried. It was too hot for him to hold.

"Ray! Ray, we need your help, man!" Big John called.

"Come on, Majors!" Zimmer yelled.

As soon as Zimmer said it, time stopped. Big John froze mid-reload, his eyes wide. Ray's mind cleared like a fog lifting, and his heart quit mid-beat.

Zimmer had called him Majors on the battlefield.

The moment broke like lightning. Japanese rifles and machine gun tracers mowed down the Okinawans from behind and pelted the ridgeline. The Japanese poured everything they had at the saddle between the hills.

And then a grenade landed right between Ray's legs.

"Run, run! Get out of here!" Big John roared.

Ray launched himself from the saddle. He dove behind a tree stump as the grenade exploded behind him, and he tumbled head over heels down the hill. He landed with a crunching thud, his ears ringing from the nearness of the blast, his helmet gone. He didn't know if Big John or Zimmer or the new guy were still alive, and he didn't turn around to find out.

Ray staggered to his feet and ran, ran straight and low and fast just like Sergeant Meredith had taught him. He didn't know where he was, or where he was going. He just knew he never wanted to see another Japanese soldier again as long as he lived.

BOOM

Hideki ran.

He dodged shattered trees. Leaped over corpses. Ducked mortar explosions. He was close to the front line—he could tell from the gunfire, the explosions that shook the earth. He knew he should stop. Turn around. Find a place to hide. But he couldn't stop himself. He was more scared than he had ever been in his entire life. He had to get as far away from the Americans as fast as he could.

He had to run. Had to keep going.

There was no going back. Only forward.

Ray ran.

He dodged shattered trees. Leaped over corpses.

Ducked mortar explosions. He was getting farther from the front line—he could tell from the distant gunfire, the dull thud of the explosions. He knew he should stop. Turn around. Rejoin his company. But he couldn't stop himself. He was more scared than he had ever been in his entire life. He had to get as far away from the Japanese as fast as he could.

He had to run. He had to keep going.

Stay low. Don't bunch up. Run like hell.

Hideki crested a low hill and slid down the other side. He'd run too far without zigging. Too far without zagging. Too far straight ahead. At the bottom of the hill he changed direction and took a hard-right turn, running straight for a stunted little pine tree that had miraculously escaped all the shells falling on the island. He ran left around the tree—

Ray slid down a low hill and struggled up the other side. He'd run zigzag too far, like a chicken trying to escape a fox. At the top of the hill he stopped dodging back and forth and ran straight ahead, toward a stunted little pine tree that had miraculously escaped all the shells falling on the island. He ran right around the tree—

Hideki slammed into someone bigger and stronger running the other way. It was like running headlong into a stone wall, and he landed with a *splurch* in the mud.

Ray hit somebody small and fast coming the other way around the tree. The boy's helmet hit him right in the gut like a punch to the stomach, and he fell back into the mud with a *splurch*.

Hideki was dazed for a moment, but when he shook off his surprise, he found himself staring at a young man wearing an American soldier's uniform.

Ray was equally dazed, and when he got his breath back, he found himself staring at a young boy wearing a Japanese soldier's uniform.

A moment passed—an eternity of shock and fear condensed into the single beat of a heart—and they both scrambled back away from each other.

Ray fumbled for his rifle.

Hideki scrabbled for a grenade.

Ray raised his rifle from the mud.

Hideki struck the fuse on his grenade.

Ray squeezed the trigger of his M-1.

Hideki threw his grenade.

Pakow!

BOOM!

The blast threw Ray and Hideki back into the mud and knocked them both out cold.

PART TWO

THE SOLDIER

Hideki woke to rain slapping him in the face. His head was groggy, and he couldn't focus his eyes. He ran a hand through his hair and felt something wet and sticky. Blood. Where was he? How had he been injured? Why was he lying on his back in the mud? And why were his ears ringing?

The cave. He remembered the cave, and the crazy lieutenant. His arm still stung from the gunshot. Hideki remembered the air shaft. The flamethrower. Running. Running and running and running and then—

The soldier. The grenade.

Hideki propped himself up on his elbows. As his focus returned, he saw the body of the American soldier lying just beyond the pine tree a few yards away. Hideki's heart hammered in his chest. What if the soldier was still alive? He wasn't moving now, but what if he woke up?

Hideki scrambled back, away from the soldier. But the American still wasn't moving, even as the rain beat down on his upturned face. Hideki stood and crept around the other side of the pine tree, his legs wobbly, afraid that any moment the soldier was going to jerk awake and start shooting at him again.

But the American soldier wasn't going to get up ever again.

The American soldier was dead.

Hideki's quaking legs gave way, and he plopped back down into the mud. He had killed a man. *He had killed a man.* Back at school, when he'd first been given his grenades, he'd been excited at the thought of blowing up an American soldier. And this one had even shot at him. But now that Hideki had done it, now that he had actually taken another human being's life, he felt a great yawning emptiness inside. A shaking sadness came over him, and he wept. He didn't care about being brave anymore. Or defending the Emperor. Or fighting the Americans. He just wanted to undo what he'd done. To take it back.

But the soldier's broken body told him there was no going back.

How could he move forward from this? His life was now divided in two—the time before he threw his grenade, and the time after it. How would he ever be the boy he was before? How could he go on?

The zipping bullets and thundering mortar shells that exploded all around him answered that question. He had to move on, or die.

His stomach in knots, Hideki crawled toward the body of the American soldier. He was surprised to see that the soldier wasn't much older than he was. More a freckle-faced boy than a man. He didn't even have the beginnings of a beard. Hideki felt sick all over again for killing him.

"I'm sorry," Hideki told the boy, but of course the boy didn't answer back. He just kept looking up lifelessly into the sky.

Hideki noticed the boy's pack and realized he'd be a fool to leave behind whatever was inside. He wrestled the pack from the body, turning the boy's face down into the mud. Hiding those questioning, frightened eyes for good.

Hideki was about to steal the dead boy's shoes too—they looked like they would fit—when he caught a flash of movement from the corner of his eye. He spun, panicking—but there was no one there. He turned this way and that, sure someone was with him, but all he saw was the driving rain, and all he heard was the hammering of his own heart.

Feeling guilty and frightened, Hideki snatched up the American's backpack and ran.

GHOSTS

Hideki hiked the soldier's pack up on his shoulders and went back down the other side of the hill. Where was he going again? *South.* Yes, that's where he was going. Through the front lines to Ichinichibashi. To find his sister. It was hard to think straight after the explosion. Hideki's head throbbed, and his eyes were still blurry. His bare feet were clammy and sore. He needed to get someplace safe and dry where he could lie down first. Close his eyes. Find something to eat.

American tracer fire streaked across the sky, red lines that crisscrossed the low, gray storm clouds. Artillery shells from both sides shook the ground. Mud filled the cratered fields, and every tree was shattered and broken.

It felt like the end of the world.

Hideki staggered into what looked like an old Japanese camp. Sandbags were stacked up in a ring, and a torn canvas lean-to tent was tied to what was left of a tree. Hideki guessed the IJA had abandoned the place before they were overrun by American soldiers.

Hideki scavenged through the camp, looking for food. His eyes fell on cardboard ration boxes half buried in the mud and he dropped to his knees to dig them up. The boxes had food in them, but it was all spoiled. The Japanese soldiers had deliberately destroyed them so they wouldn't fall into enemy hands. A whole crate full of food, ruined!

Hideki sobbed once, then dragged himself wearily into the partial shelter of the lean-to. It was muddy and wet under the torn tarp, but at least it kept the rain from pounding his sore head. Hideki shrugged off the heavy American army pack and planted it at his feet. It was time to see what was inside.

Hideki set aside the shovel attached to the outside of the pack. He would keep that. The other items he examined one by one. Extra socks: keep, for if he ever found shoes again. Toothpaste and toothbrush: throw away. Matches and lighter: keep. Japanese money: That was a surprise. Keep. What looked like an English-to-Japanese phrase book: throw away. Cigarettes: keep. Hideki didn't smoke, but plenty of Japanese soldiers did. He might be able to trade the cigarettes for food. Razor and shaving cream: Not even the young soldier had needed this, so why had he lugged them around with him? Hideki threw them away.

Hideki was disappointed not to find any medicine or bandages he could use on his head and his arm and his scraped-up elbows and knees. He thought again about the dead American soldier, and he shuddered. Hideki pushed the image of the soldier down, trying to forget it, but he knew he never would.

Hideki dug deeper in the pack and came to thin cardboard boxes that looked like the ones Japanese army meals came in. Hideki tore open one of the packages. Inside were neat little paper-covered rectangular packets, hard crackers, and something brick-like covered in aluminum foil. There was also a tin can and a key to open it.

Food! It had to be! Everything had English words on it to explain what it was, but Hideki couldn't read any of it. Hideki's stomach snarled at him. He wanted to rip open the packets and eat whatever it was, but he hesitated. For months the Japanese army had told him and all the other Okinawans that the American devils couldn't be trusted. That they would lure them in with the promise of food, only to trick them. What if the English words on one of these packets said POISON and he ate it? He would have fallen right into their trap.

Almost crying, Hideki put the lid back on the

cardboard box and stuffed it back down inside the pack. He wouldn't eat it. But he wouldn't throw it away either. If he was about to die from starvation, he would try the food. By that point, what would he have to lose? But while he could still stand, could still stagger on, he would wait.

As Hideki repacked the bag, he found a waxen, waterproof pocket he hadn't seen before. Inside was a stack of photographs. They were black-and-white, with a glossy, slick feel to them on the picture side and thick, coarse paper on the backs.

The first picture was of an American boy and a man who must have been his father, dressed up in funny costumes.

It wasn't just *any* American boy, Hideki realized. It was *the* boy. The one Hideki had killed. The American soldier before he was a soldier, when he was younger even than Hideki. Hideki felt like he was looking at a ghost, and he got goose bumps.

Hideki quickly shuffled the picture to the back of the stack.

The next picture surprised him. It wasn't of the boy or his family, or of any American. It was a photograph of a Japanese soldier, in uniform, sitting with a woman in a kimono under a cherry tree. His girlfriend or his wife, Hideki guessed. On the back, someone had written *Kanazawa, 1944* in Japanese. Hideki looked at the photo for a long time. The couple must have been on a *hanami* picnic—a flower-viewing picnic. In Japan and Okinawa, people gathered each year with their families and friends to sit under the cherry trees when they bloomed. The picture was black-and-white, but Hideki could imagine the vibrant pink colors of the blossoms, the bright blue sky. What were they saying to each other, this young man and young woman? Were they planning their lives together? What happened right after the picture was taken? Did they lie back under the trees, holding hands as they stared up into the sky? Did they kiss?

The rest of the pictures were of more Japanese people. Some were Japanese soldiers. Others were women and young children, or older couples who looked like mothers and fathers. Some had places or names written on the back in *kanji*: *Sapporo, Nagasaki, Osaka, Tokyo. Mother and Father, Hisako and Mieko, Futoshi and Toyo.* Why did an American soldier have these pictures in his pack?

The last picture made Hideki freeze. His eyes widened. He knew this picture. It was the photograph from the wall of his sister's school! The one he'd seen an American soldier take from its frame while Hideki was in the same room, pretending to be dead! *This* American soldier—the boy Hideki had killed. They had been in the same room together, long before they had run into each other on the battlefield. One of the other soldiers had used the American's name when he called to him. What was it? Hideki's head was so foggy he couldn't remember.

This soldier had been keeping all these pictures the same way Principal Kojima had carried the pictures of the Emperor. Did Americans know about *mabui*? Was this soldier carrying the pictures with him so these people's spirits would be protected and preserved? Hideki hadn't thought the Americans would care about things like that. Especially not the *mabui* of their enemies. The Americans were supposed to be devils. Evil.

Hideki flipped back to the picture of the boy and his father and studied their faces. They didn't look evil. But what did evil really look like, after all? Evil was what you did, not how you appeared on the outside.

"Rei," Hideki said aloud. That's what the other soldier had called the boy. It came back to him through the fog.

Rei was the name of the boy Hideki had killed.

The air grew cold, and Hideki's skin crawled. He had the singular sensation that he was being watched, but when he looked around, he was alone.

With a shiver, Hideki suddenly remembered: *rei* was another word in Japanese for "ghost."

ONE WAY OUT

Hideki was so thirsty he tried to catch rainwater in his mouth, but it wasn't enough. He searched until he found a rivulet of running water in the darkness. The water was muddy and foul, and who knew where it came from and what was in it, but Hideki drank it anyway. He didn't know how far he'd wandered, or how long. All he knew was that his head still pounded, his stomach still growled, and Shuri Castle still stood.

Someone splashed through the muck nearby, and Hideki reached for his last grenade. The person was bent over and carried something big and round on his back. Was it another American soldier? No—he was too small for that. The shadowy figure drew closer, and Hideki saw it was an older Okinawan boy. On his back he carried a small wooden barrel.

The boy saw Hideki at almost the same moment, and he cried out in surprise, falling backward onto his barrel.

"I'm sorry!" Hideki said. "I'm sorry—I'm Okinawan too. I didn't mean to scare you."

"Hideki?" the other boy asked.

Hideki was startled. Was this somebody he knew?

"Hideki, it's Yoshio," the boy said.

Hideki reeled. *Yoshio?* Yoshio was only a year older than him, but this boy looked like he was ten years older. Yoshio's face was hollow and thin, with deep bags of sleeplessness under his eyes. Yoshio had changed so much in just a few weeks. With a sudden jolt, Hideki wondered if he had too.

Yoshio splashed across the water toward him. Hideki flinched, expecting a punch, but Yoshio threw his arms around Hideki instead. Yoshio was . . . hugging him? Hideki stood rigid, expecting a trick, but Yoshio just clapped him on the shoulders.

"Hideki, it's so good to see you! I thought you died when we attacked the Americans."

"I—I thought you were dead too," Hideki said. Yoshio smiled like they were the best of friends. Like Yoshio hadn't tormented him constantly for the past four years. What was going on here?

"What are you doing with that barrel?" Hideki asked him.

"Getting water for my family. Hideki, I found my mother and sister! Can you believe it?"

It was incredible, yes, but Hideki had found his own father too. It was a small island, after all. But the mention of Yoshio's mother and sister made Hideki's heart ache for his dead mother and brother. For a moment he was lost in a vision of them in the dark, treading water, trying not to slip under the waves, until Yoshio's voice brought him back to the present.

"We're hiding in a cave nearby! Do you need a dry place to sleep?" Yoshio asked. "Help me fill this barrel, and I'll take you back there!"

Hideki was still wary of Yoshio's friendliness, but he helped the boy lug the water barrel back to the cave where his family was hiding. He and Yoshio were met at the entrance by an Okinawan woman and a little girl—Yoshio's mother and sister—and an elderly man and woman who helped them haul the barrel inside. There were more Okinawans deeper inside the cave too.

From the reek of human excrement and sweat, Hideki guessed that most of them hadn't left the cave since the battle began. Even so, Hideki was relieved to finally be out of the rain and among his own people. But as his eyes adjusted to the darkness of the cave, he saw something that turned his empty stomach.

There was a Japanese soldier here too.

Hideki took a step back toward the entrance of the cave, but Yoshio was too fast for him.

"This is my friend Hideki, from school!" Yoshio told everyone. He put an arm around Hideki and gave him a playful squeeze.

Friend? Since when were they friends?

"I was just helping Yoshio bring the barrel back," Hideki explained. He backed away from Yoshio. "I won't take up any of your space."

"No!" the Japanese soldier cried. He ran to block Hideki's way out of the cave. "You can't go! It's not safe. There are Americans everywhere!" There was a nervous twitch in his cheek, and his hands shook like he was freezing. He peered nervously through the cave's small entrance. "Did anyone follow you back?" he demanded, his eyes big.

"No," Hideki said. He was tired. So very, very tired. And now he had another unhinged Japanese soldier to deal with. One had tried to force him out to fight against the Americans, and this one wouldn't let him leave. Hideki put his head in his hands. All he wanted was to lie down. Close his eyes. Escape the constant pulsing in his ears.

"I—I don't understand," Yoshio whispered to Hideki. "Private Maeda wasn't like this yesterday."

Yesterday they probably had more food, Hideki thought. Weeks inside this stinking cave with bombs falling outside and dwindling food and water had driven Private Maeda close to his breaking point.

Before the Americans had invaded, Hideki had known the Japanese soldiers to be demanding taskmasters. But they had never been crazy. Not like this. The war had changed Yoshio somehow for the better, and it had changed soldiers like Private Maeda for the worse.

Hideki watched Private Maeda eye the door warily, and wondered how long it would be until the soldier turned that suspicious look on the Okinawans.

Hideki fought the fog in his head and scanned the cave, looking for any other way out. But the only one he could see was through the front entrance, past Private Maeda. Would Maeda shoot him if he tried to leave? Was there any way he could slip past him?

The water barrel. Private Maeda had sent Yoshio out tonight to refill the water barrel, and he would send some other expendable Okinawan out to refill it tomorrow. That was how Hideki would get out. The next time they needed a water boy, he would volunteer to go, and he would never come back.

A CIGARETTE FOR REI

Hideki ran through fire, chased by a cackling *kijimunaa*. *Kijimunaa* were little naked forest sprites with big heads and flaming red hair. Hideki zigged and zagged, but he couldn't escape it. Then the pine tree loomed up ahead of him again, and again there was nowhere to turn. Hideki knew what was coming, what waited for him around the other side of that pine tree, but he couldn't stop, couldn't stop. And suddenly there he was. The American soldier. Rei. Hideki barreled into him, and then the dream exploded with the force of a grenade.

"Ahhhh! No! No! I'm sorry!" Hideki cried. He shot straight up, his chest tight, his face covered in sweat.

The others in the cave around him woke up, grumbling, and then turned over to go back to sleep.

"Keep that boy quiet, or I'll make him quiet!"

Private Maeda hissed from his guard post at the front of the cave.

Hideki ran a hand over his face. He had a fever, he was sure of it, and he shivered even though he was burning up inside.

"Here, my dear," an old Okinawan woman whispered, making him jump. The woman's face was wrinkled, and she wore a matching blue *bashōfu* kimono and kerchief. She had brought Hideki a cup of dirty water from the water barrel he and Yoshio had carried back to the cave.

As Hideki nodded his thanks and took the cup from the kind old lady, he noticed the backs of her hands. They were tattooed with *hajichi*. *Hajichi* were indigo tattoos Okinawan women had once worn on the backs of their hands to mark important events in their lives. The Japanese government had banned *hajichi* long before Hideki was born, but some old women still had them. Hideki caught glimpses of a circle and square that represented a wound spool of thread and a sewing box, arrows that marked the days her daughters left home to start families of their own, and little stars for when her grandchildren had been born. Then the old woman's hands disappeared inside the sleeves of her kimono.

"Did you have a nightmare?" the old woman asked. She spoke Okinawan, not Japanese.

"I was being chased by a *kijimunaa*," Hideki whispered.

The old woman nodded. "There are many *kijimunaa* about these days. Their homes in the banyan trees are all destroyed. They usually hate the smell of farts though, so I don't know what they're doing in this stinky cave."

She was trying to cheer him up, but Hideki's despair went deeper than fart jokes. He avoided her eyes and stared into the dark water in his cup.

"There's something more though, isn't there?" the old woman asked.

Hideki could still feel the weight of it on his chest. "I—I killed a man. An American soldier. And I think . . . I think he's haunting me. I've been seeing things. Hearing things . . ."

The old woman looked at Hideki this way and that, as though trying to spot a spider that was crawling on him. "No—this is no *yōkai*. You have the American's *mabui* on you."

Hideki gave a start. *He carried Rei's* mabui*?* How did she know? But then Hideki remembered his grandmother, back when she was alive, helping Hideki find his own *mabui* every day after he'd lost it playing outside. Maybe you had to be older to see it.

"I thought you could only carry the *mabui* of an ancestor," Hideki said.

"Oh, no," said the woman. "A person's *mabui* can come loose when something shocking happens.

Sometimes a *mabui* is simply lost, and you can find it again. But sometimes it attaches itself to someone else. Was his death a particularly frightful one?"

Hideki saw himself running into Rei. Knocking him down. Fumbling for his grenade. Throwing it.

"Yes," Hideki said. His heart sank. Not only had he killed Rei, he had done it in so shocking a manner that Rei's very spirit had come unstuck and attached to him. No wonder he'd felt haunted. It wasn't just Shigetomo's *mabui* that was competing with Hideki's soul. It was Rei's too.

"Can you help me get rid of it?" Hideki asked the old woman.

She shook her head. "For that you need a *yuta*."

Kimiko. Hideki was already going to find his sister, and now he was even more eager to reach her. If he could just clear this fog from his head. And get past Private Maeda and his rifle. Then he could help Kimiko and Kimiko could help him.

But it might be days before he found her. Weeks.

If she was even still alive.

"Maybe I can do it myself," Hideki said. Kimiko had taught Hideki how to perform the ceremony to try to appease Shigetomo's *mabui*. Shigetomo's spirit had proven too stubborn to go away with just a ritual, but maybe it would work with Rei's.

Hideki remembered the words, but he didn't have

incense. No—wait! He did have something. He dug in Rei's pack and pulled out the matches and cigarettes. He could light the cigarettes and use them as incense. And they had even belonged to the dead soldier. That had to help.

Hideki lit one of the cigarettes and fanned it until a trickle of smoke rose from it. In something like a fever dream, Hideki closed his eyes and began to speak to Rei's *mabui*.

"I'm sorry, Rei," Hideki said. "I didn't know what I was doing. I was afraid, and my fear turned me into a monster."

The trick was for Hideki and Rei to come to some sort of understanding about what had happened. To resolve whatever issues Rei's *mabui* still had with the way he had died.

Hideki felt a chill, and when he opened his eyes, he thought he could almost see the American standing there in front of him in the smoke.

"*Rei*," Hideki whispered.

"What's that smell?"

Private Maeda's angry voice broke the spell. The scent of burning tobacco had drawn him to the back of the cave. The private waved away the smoke and picked up the cigarette, ruining everything.

"This is an American cigarette! Where did you get this?" Maeda demanded. He tossed the cigarette on the floor and and snatched up Rei's pack. "This is an American pack! Are you a spy?"

"What? No!" Hideki said. "I took it off a soldier I killed!"

The others in the cave awoke to the yelling, and Hideki heard them murmuring and stirring around him.

"The boy is just trying to appease the spirit of the man who died," the old woman told the soldier. She said it in Okinawan though, not Japanese, and it threw the soldier into a rage.

"You were told to speak only Japanese!" Maeda yelled. "Anyone who doesn't speak Japanese is the enemy!"

"She's an old lady who doesn't speak Japanese," Hideki tried to explain. "She was just telling you what I was doing with the cigarettes."

But the private wasn't listening. "What are you trying to hide?" he yelled at the old woman. He yanked her up by the arm, and her kimono fell away from her hands. When the soldier saw her markings, his eyes went wide.

"These tattoos—they are forbidden! You are Okinawan spies, both of you!" With his other hand, the soldier grabbed Hideki's arm. Private Maeda dragged him and the old woman toward the mouth of the cave. "Spies and traitors will be shot!"

SPIES

"No! Please! Wait!" Hideki cried. "Yoshio! Somebody! Help us!"

Yoshio was awake and sitting up, but he didn't leave his mother's side. None of the other Okinawans moved to help Hideki and the old woman. No one wanted to draw the crazy soldier's attention.

As Maeda wrestled both of them toward the entrance of the cave, Hideki remembered the grenade in his pocket. His last grenade. He pulled it out and uncorked the rubber stopper.

"I have a grenade!" Hideki cried. "Let us go, or I'll blow us all up!"

Private Maeda released Hideki and the old woman. He stepped back, frightened. Hideki's heart raced. He couldn't believe what he was doing. But what other choice did he have?

Private Maeda's rifle was propped up against the wall a few steps away. He glanced at it, then back at the grenade, then took a step toward his rifle.

"Don't!" Hideki said. He brought the fuse and the cap closer like he was about to light the grenade, and Maeda froze. "We're not spies," Hideki tried to explain again. "I took those cigarettes—I took those cigarettes from a dead American soldier." The blood was thundering in his aching head, and he was having trouble putting words together. Remembering how to speak Japanese. "I'm in the Blood and Iron Student Corps," Hideki told Private Maeda. "I was just trying to get rid of the *mabui* of the man I killed."

"What's a '*mabui*'? I don't even know what that means!" the soldier yelled.

"What's happening?" the old woman asked Hideki in Okinawan. "Why is he angry with us?"

"Spies!" Maeda cried again. "Anyone who speaks Okinawan is a spy!"

Hideki knew then that nothing he said would satisfy the private. Maeda was angry and hungry and scared, and as long as there were American soldiers on Okinawa, as long as American bombs kept falling all day and all night, nothing was going to change that.

Private Maeda took another step toward his rifle.

Hideki snatched up the still-smoldering cigarette from the floor of the cave and held it close to the grenade fuse.

"If you touch that rifle, I'll light this fuse," Hideki promised. As he said it, visions of Rei at the pine tree flooded back to him—Rei raising his rifle, Hideki lighting his grenade. The shot. The explosion. Hideki felt a cold shiver go down his back, saw a shadow flicker out of the corner of his eye. He didn't turn to look at it though. He knew what it was.

Who it was.

"I've killed a man," Hideki said quietly. "Have you?"

That seemed to get through to Maeda at last. Sweat broke out on his forehead and he slowly lifted his arms in surrender.

"Move to the back of the cave," Hideki told him.

Maeda did, his eyes never leaving the grenade. The Okinawans in the back of the cave slid away from the private, keeping their distance from Hideki too. Yoshio stared at Hideki with wide, disbelieving eyes.

"Come with me," Hideki said.

"Who? Me?" the old woman asked. She stepped deeper into the cave, away from Hideki.

"All of you," Hideki said. His eyes flitted from Maeda to the Okinawans and back again, but he spoke to the families in the corner. "This man has gone crazy. It's not safe here any longer. Come with me."

"Where?" asked one of the old Okinawan men. "It's

not safe outside either! We can feel the bombs. Hear the guns."

The old man was right. Hideki knew it. They shouldn't stay here, but they shouldn't come with him, either. Nowhere on Okinawa was safe for Okinawans.

Hideki bent down and slipped his arm through one of the straps on Rei's pack, quickly bringing the smoking cigarette back up to the fuse. The weight of the pack threw off his coordination, and he almost touched the burning ember to the fuse by accident. Private Maeda cried out and cowered, but the grenade wasn't lit.

Hideki backed away toward the entrance. He was going to be on his own again.

"These people are not spies," Hideki told Maeda. "They are innocent Japanese citizens who need your help. Your protection. But since I don't trust you to keep them safe, I'm taking *this*."

Hideki snatched up Private Maeda's rifle and dashed out into the rain.

FADING AWAY

Hideki heard Private Maeda yell out behind him, but he didn't slow down to look back. Once he was outside the cave, he zigzagged this way and that for the cover of a low hill in the distance.

It was cloudy and rainy but it was daylight out now, and the water and the light in his eyes blinded him. His heart pounded like a hammer as he slipped and slid, juggling the grenade, the pack, and the rifle. The cigarette had already been drowned in the rain, and he let it fall into the mud.

Hideki ran and ran, but unlike the *kijimunaa* that chased Hideki in his dreams, Private Maeda didn't follow him. At the edge of a steep ridge, Hideki flung the private's rifle down, down into the ravine, where it sank into the mud with a *splurch*. He never once considered keeping it. Just carrying a rifle was dangerous. People with rifles shot at other people with rifles, and he didn't know how to use the thing anyway.

Yoshio and the old woman and the other Okinawans in the cave might still not be safe, but at least now they couldn't be shot by Private Maeda.

Hideki kept running. When his lungs gave out, he collapsed underneath the remains of an exploded American tank. He panted heavily, his body still weak from days with too little food and too little sleep, his head still ringing. He stuffed the unused grenade back in his pocket. How many other brushes with death would it help him escape from?

Hideki wanted to go on, to look for Kimiko, but he felt himself fading. He was crashing from the adrenaline rush of his standoff with Private Maeda, from running away. His escape had used up the last of his energy, and his sick, feverish body was giving up. If he didn't eat some food today—*real* food—he was going to die.

It was time to try the food in Rei's backpack.

Hideki tried one of the hard, unwrapped crackers first. It was tough to bite off, and it tasted like wood shavings, but Hideki was able to gulp it down. He wanted to wait, to see if the cracker was poisoned and would make him sick, but his hunger got the better of him. He bit off more and more, swallowing the dry bits of cracker as fast as he could choke them down. The second, third, and fourth crackers quickly followed the first. If they *were* poison, he was at least going to die with a full belly.

The can with the key might have food in it too. Better food than the crackers. But what if it was some kind of an explosive device instead that would blow up in Hideki's face? Surely he'd eaten enough crackers to buy him another couple of days. But his body still shook with hunger and the anticipation of what might be inside the can. He would try it. He had to. Eyes closed, head turned, Hideki snapped the key into the can's lid and cranked it back.

The smell that rose from the can made his mouth water. It wasn't an explosive device, it was *potatoes and beef.* Real meat! In a daze, Hideki used the fork from the meal kit to spear a piece of beef. His hand shook as he lifted the morsel to his mouth, afraid he would drop it. Afraid it might somehow go away or be taken from him at the last moment.

He placed a mouthful on his tongue and closed his eyes. It tasted overwhelmingly of salt, but underneath it was the fatty, rich flavor of beef, something Hideki hadn't tasted since long before the battle began. Hideki chewed the meat slowly and fought his stomach's powerful urge to swallow it down quickly.

Hideki's eyes watered at the sheer joy of it, and he cried softly. The food was so good, and it had taken him so long to eat it. He might even have lost the pack before he'd tried it. And the food hadn't been poisoned after all.

It took all the willpower he had, but Hideki saved the rest for later. He would need it. His stomach still yawned, begging for more food, but he had bought himself more time. He felt solid again. Less like a ghost. He repacked Rei's bag, took off his clammy, wet jacket, and put both of them under his head for a pillow. His head still pounded, and he needed to close his eyes. To rest.

In seconds, Hideki was asleep. He twisted and turned, his body still blazing with fever and shaking with hunger, and as he slept he dreamed. He was being chased by a *kijimunaa* again. The *kijimunaa* hurled pinecones at him that exploded like grenades, cratering the ground to Hideki's left and right. Hideki ran and ran, through rice paddies and around trees, up hills and over streams. But every time he turned to look over his shoulder, the *kijimunaa* was right there behind him, cackling and hurling more pinecone grenades at him. *Boom. Boom. Boom. Boom.*

The evil sprite was chasing him toward the pine tree again, toward Rei, but this time the *kijimunaa* caught him first. It leaped onto his back and sank its long, sharp fangs into his neck, and Hideki jerked awake.

He blinked in confusion. Hideki wasn't where he

had gone to sleep. The blown-up tank, the muddy field, the pouring rain—they were all gone. He lay instead on a cot under a green army tent. A green *American* army tent.

Hideki had been captured by the enemy.

THINGS THAT AREN'T THERE

Hideki was a prisoner of the Americans! He turned to roll off his cot, to run away, but a man stood over him, silhouetted by the dawn. Hideki lifted a hand to shade his eyes.

It was Rei. Rei, the boy he'd killed, was standing over him, a gaping hole in his side. Hideki's heart caught in his throat, and he sat up with a yelp.

Suddenly, the ghost of Rei was gone, and an American doctor stepped into the space where Rei had once stood. Or had he? Hideki blinked and put a hand to his sore head—but instead of touching dried blood he found a gauze bandage there, wrapped tight.

"You're all right," the American doctor said. It took Hideki a confused moment to realize the medic was speaking Japanese. The doctor handed Hideki two small white pills and a metal cup of water. "Here. Swallow these. They will make you feel better," the doctor told him.

Hideki put a hand to the place on his neck where the *kijimunaa* had bitten him. A small cloth bandage covered the spot.

"I had to give you a shot to help you sleep," the doctor explained. "You had a nasty gash on your head, and we had to sew it up for you. It's still going to hurt for a while though, and these pills will help."

Hideki was afraid of the pills. But why would the Americans go to all the trouble of fixing him if they were just going to poison him now? He put the two pills in his mouth. They tasted like chalk, and he quickly swallowed them down with the water.

"Good boy," the doctor said. "It looks like shrapnel from a grenade caught you. What happened?"

Hideki felt the blood drain from his face. He couldn't tell the doctor what really happened—that he'd been injured by his own grenade killing an American soldier. Killing Rei.

"I—I don't remember," Hideki lied.

"That may be a result of the concussion," he told Hideki. "You may have problems with your memory, or problems with your eyes and ears, like hearing and seeing things that aren't there."

Hearing and seeing things that aren't there. Was that

what was happening to Hideki? Was he hearing and seeing Rei because he'd taken a knock to the head, or because Rei's ghost was haunting him?

"Get some rest," the doctor told him, "and maybe your memory will come back to you. In the meantime, I'll see if I can find you some shoes that fit you."

When the doctor was gone, Hideki snatched a bottle of the little white pills from a tray and stuffed the bottle in his pocket. Then he got up from the cot and slipped out of the medical tent. All around the camp, American doctors and soldiers walked on boards laid down in the mud, and trucks unloaded more Okinawans, both injured and uninjured. None of them seemed to be prisoners.

First the food in Rei's pack hadn't been poisoned, and now the Americans had treated his wounds. He'd seen them be monsters, but he'd seen them be kind too. Maybe it wouldn't be so bad to surrender to them after all. But if the Americans ever found out what he'd done to Rei, they might not be so nice.

Besides, he had his sister to find.

NO-MAN'S-LAND

American star shells exploded in the sky above Hideki. Designed not to kill but to illuminate, the shells burst into bright glowing stars that hung from tiny parachutes. It took the star shells about a minute to hit the ground, and in that time everything below them was lit up with a ghostly green light.

For Hideki, it was like the Americans were lighting his way south, toward his sister. But it was also the way toward the dangerous front lines, where the Americans and Japanese were still fighting.

After a quick detour to pick up Rei's pack, Hideki had joined hundreds of Okinawan refugees walking in the same direction. He hoped the Americans would let him pass through safely with the refugees, and then he could press on farther south to find Kimiko.

The Americans used illumination shells to watch for Japanese infiltrators at night. What the light showed Hideki and the other refugees were all the dead bodies around them. Some were Japanese, but most were Okinawan. They littered the muddy fields to each side and lay like stones in the road. But Hideki had learned to not really see them and keep moving. Seeing them—*really* seeing them—was too much to bear.

Hideki felt the skin on the back of his neck crawl, like the person behind him was breathing on him, and he spun. But the nearest person was four steps away. Hideki shivered and turned to walk again. Was it the ghost of Rei? The ghost of his father? It was hard to know. It could have been the ghost of any of the thousands of other people who had died on Okinawa since the fighting began. The reek of death was everywhere.

Another star shell exploded in the sky, and Hideki looked down at his cold, sodden feet. He was just thinking that maybe he should have waited until the American doctor brought back shoes for him when he noticed the shoes underneath the *bashōfu* kimono of the woman walking next to him. They weren't wooden sandals or *tabi* socks. They were leather boots. The woman wasn't a woman at all—"she" was a Japanese soldier wearing a kimono over his uniform!

A quick scan of the feet all around him found more army boots hidden among the kimonos. Japanese soldiers had snuck in among their ranks throughout the night, hoping to slip through enemy lines with the refugees.

Hideki's heart skipped a beat. He was in trouble. They all were. When American soldiers discovered there were Japanese soldiers hiding among them, the Americans would kill them all. But if he said anything now, raised the alarm, the Japanese soldiers would just as likely kill them all as spies.

Hideki slipped off the road, away from the refugees. He had walked straight with them for far too long. Evil was about to catch up to these people on both sides.

Zigging and zagging, Hideki used the eerily illuminated Shuri Castle as a landmark and made his way further south on his own. He thought again about the cave with Yoshio and Private Maeda and the old woman. Were the Okinawans safe? Did Private Maeda still think the old woman was a spy? And what about Yoshio? How had he gone from being Hideki's worst enemy to Hideki's best friend? Not that he had come to Hideki's defense when Private Maeda went crazy. But what could Yoshio have done, really? What could any of the Okinawans do against the Americans and the Japanese?

Hideki slid to the bottom of a steep ravine, where a body lay half-buried in the mud. Another star shell exploded overhead, and in the light Hideki saw that the fallen soldier was an American. That was unusual. The Americans usually claimed their casualties as soon as they could, taking them away to treat them or bury them. It was the Japanese who couldn't come out of their defensive bunkers to claim their dead.

Hideki knelt by the body and went through the man's pack. There was food! And a photograph. A pretty woman wearing a dress and sitting on a beach. The smeared imprint of her red lips decorated the bottom corner of the photo.

There were more American bodies nearby, and Hideki hurriedly stuffed his own pack with as much food as he could find from theirs. He kept all the pictures he found too, adding them to Rei's collection. *Their* collection now.

A single shot rang out—*pakow*—and a bullet *fwipped* into the mud near Hideki. A sniper! Hideki dove behind one of the bodies. The sniper didn't shoot again, but he knew where Hideki was. Hideki cursed himself for his stupidity. There was a reason this ravine was still full of American corpses. It was too dangerous to come and get them! He must have wandered right into the no-man's-land between the Americans on one side, and the Japanese on the other.

That meant that the slope behind him was occupied by the Imperial Japanese Army. If he could get to one of the caves inside it, he'd be safe. But if he stood, the American sniper would have a clear shot again.

Hideki watched the star shell overhead growing

dimmer and dimmer. He waited, his throat dry with anticipation, until the shell suddenly winked out and everything was pitch-black again. Hideki leaped to his feet and ran up the hill, his bare feet slipping in the mud beneath him. For every meter he gained he felt like he lost a half meter sliding back down.

Pakow. Pakow. Pakow. Bullets *fwipped* into the hillside around him. The American sniper couldn't see him, but he knew Hideki would be running in the darkness. Hideki climbed faster, his arms and legs scrambling to push him higher. Higher. *Pakow. Pakow-pakow.* More rifles joined the first. The American sentries were taking pot shots at him, hoping to hit him in the dark.

P-poom. A battleship offshore fired another star shell. It whistled high into the air, leaving a glowing green-white trail. Any second now it would explode, the burning phosphorus lighting up the whole hillside. The American snipers would see him plain as day.

Hideki's hand hit something wooden. A man-made ledge.

Fwasssh. The star shell burst overhead, and Hideki saw a small open window cut into the hillside, just big enough for him to crawl through.

And the Americans saw *him.*

Hideki tossed his backpack into the hole as bullets shredded the wooden frame, then pulled himself through the window headfirst. He hit the rock floor inside with a thump and scrambled back against the wall as bullets pinged through the opening. He licked his dry lips and panted hard, but at least he was still breathing. He'd made it!

But where were the Japanese? The bunker was empty. If the Americans had been charging this hill for days and couldn't even come close enough to collect their dead, where were the Japanese soldiers with their rifles and machine guns and mortars?

The American snipers stopped shooting. Hideki slid away from the hole in the wall, staying out of their line of sight. He crawled through a narrow tunnel to a larger cavern beyond, where multiple levels had been cut out of the rock. But the whole place was completely empty.

Where *was* everybody?

Hideki got goose bumps walking through the empty bunker. This place should have been teeming with Japanese soldiers. And it looked like it had been until very recently. The floors were littered with abandoned ammunition boxes, scraps of bloody bandages, and empty ration cans. But there were no people.

Hideki wound his way through the tunnels to the opposite side of the hill, facing away from the American lines. There, another hole cut in the mountain framed the scene on the other side, showing him where everyone had gone.

The Imperial Japanese Army was in full retreat. The

roads south beyond the front lines were clogged with Japanese soldiers, all hurrying toward their next line of defense under the cover of dark and rain. When the Americans attacked the hill again tomorrow, they would meet no resistance. They would storm the bunker and find no one left inside.

Except for Hideki.

Unless he left *right now.*

Hideki hiked Rei's backpack up on his shoulders, climbed through the hole, and ran.

TYPHOON OF STEEL

Hideki made a rectangle with his fingers and squinted, framing an imaginary photograph.

All around him, thousands of Okinawan refugees and Japanese soldiers trudged south in the pouring rain. The Japanese soldiers didn't even stop to go to the bathroom. They urinated as they jogged along the muddy highway, none of them willing to pause for even thirty seconds. They had to get to the next line of defensive caves before the Americans caught up.

Hidden among them, Hideki was just one of tens of thousands of people clogging the roads. The highway would take them through Shikina to Ichinichibashi, and that's as far as Hideki needed to go. Ichinichibashi was where his sister would be.

Hideki had never been this far south before, but

wherever he was, it didn't look like Okinawa anymore. American bombs had knocked down trees and taken the tops off hills, stomping the landscape flat like an angry god. Entire villages were shattered, the wooden houses and barns reduced to toothpicks. There was no color to anything anymore—the people, the ground, the sky, they were all a dull, filthy gray-brown, like all the paints on an artist's palette had been swirled together in a muddy mess. This wasn't Okinawa. Not the Okinawa that Hideki knew and loved.

Hideki had always used his fingers to frame what he was seeing in front of him, the way the photographer had taught him. But now he did something different. Now he used the frame to imagine the way Okinawa had been, before the Americans had invaded, before the Japanese army had brought in cannons and built bunkers.

He saw brilliant white coral sand roads lined with waving green palm trees. Thatched wooden barns, square houses with red terra-cotta roofs. Women in blue *bashōfu* kimonos with babies strapped to their backs, going to the market. Old men in brown *bashōfu* and round straw hats, leading water buffalo to the sugarcane fields. Everywhere he looked, the bright memory of *before* overlaid the gray, miserable *after*, like his fingers were making a window into the past, a past that was so recent, so real to him, that he could almost reach out and touch it.

Something moved in the corner of Hideki's eye, and he glanced sideways. But nothing was there.

"I know, I know," he told the ghost of Rei. "I'm sorry. I'm trying. Kimiko will be able to help us. We just have to find her first."

But how will I ever find her in all this? Hideki wondered.

An American fighter plane came roaring right up behind the long line of people, like it was following the highway. It flew so low that Hideki could make out the face of the pilot. Everyone ducked and screamed, but the plane didn't shoot at them. It roared up into the sky and circled high above them for a few seconds before disappearing into the clouds.

The Japanese soldiers among them shoved Hideki and the other Okinawans out of the way as they ran off in all directions, and Hideki suddenly understood. The plane was a spotter for the battleships offshore. It had probably already radioed in where the crowds were.

"Incoming! Get down!" Hideki yelled. He dove off the road into a water-filled ditch as the first shell exploded right in the middle of the highway.

The blast was deafening. Hideki held his breath and put his head under the water. The muffled booms shook him and rocked the ground, and he squeezed his eyes shut and drew his arms and legs in tight. Mud and rock and shrapnel pelted him. His world was hellfire and destruction for longer minutes than he could count, punctuated only by quick gasps of air.

At last the bombing stopped. Hideki waited under the water until his lungs burned so much he had to breathe, and he lifted himself up on his hands and knees.

The road was gone, and so was everyone who had been on it.

Those who had been outside the target area—those who had been spared—got to their feet and hurried on through the carnage, leaving the wounded behind.

And Hideki, his eyes dry and his heart hard, did the same.

FAMILY

It was safer to travel by night, when the American planes weren't flying and the battleships weren't shooting, but Hideki was exhausted. He had to find some place to sleep. He broke away from the refugees and soldiers plodding south and soon came to a family tomb. Hideki almost cried with relief. He staggered inside, hoping the ancestors resting there would forgive him for invading their home for one night.

But the ancestors weren't the ones he needed to worry about. The family who owned the tomb were already hiding there. There were eight of them, a mother, father, grandmother, grandfather, and four small children, all huddled in the back.

"I'm sorry," Hideki told them. "I just need to get in out of the rain. I need to sit down."

He didn't wait for them to say yes. Hideki's weary legs gave out, and he flopped to the floor of the tomb. It was all he could do to keep his eyes open. He let his pack slip off his back for the first time that day and he slumped over, absolutely exhausted.

The family crept over to meet him and introduce themselves. Their last name was Miyagi. They each told him their first names too, but Hideki was too tired to remember any of them. They had been living in this tomb since the battle began, they told him. Not one of them had been outside in two months. They still had water, but their food had run out five days ago. The littlest of the children looked shrunken, like his body was eating itself from the inside out, and they all had hollow eyes and sunken cheeks.

They look like ghosts, Hideki thought to himself. *Like their long-dead ancestors resurrected.*

Hideki thought of his father, perhaps never to be buried in the Kaneshiro family tomb, and he sagged.

"Why didn't you evacuate?" Hideki finally asked them. "Why did you stay?"

"We thought the Imperial Japanese Army would protect us," Father Miyagi said.

"This is our home," Grandfather Miyagi added. "This is where our ancestors live."

Hideki closed his eyes and nodded. It was the same answer he would have gotten from any of the refugees streaming south. *This is our home. The Japanese will protect us.* One of those things was true. The other was far from it.

"Are the Americans really coming this way?" Mother Miyagi asked Hideki.

Hideki was too tired to lie to them. "Yes," he said.

The children gasped and clutched at each other.

"Is it true what they say? That the Americans are monsters?" Father Miyagi asked.

Again, Hideki wanted to tell them the truth. But what *was* the truth?

"Yes," he told them. "And no. When they're fighting, the Americans are killing machines. When they're not, they're like us." Hideki pulled the wet tangle of bandages from his head. "One of their doctors fixed me when I was hurt," he told the Miyagis. "And they'll give you food if you ask for it."

Hideki pulled his pack around and fished out what was left of the ration boxes. They were coated with a waxy substance that helped keep them dry from the rain. The crackers were fairly disintegrated, but there was some chewy gray stuff, a few practically indestructible candy bars, and the meals in the tins. Hideki cracked one of the cans open, and Grandfather Miyagi cried out longingly at the delicious smell. Hideki took a bite to show them it was all right and offered it to the family.

"It's not poisoned," Hideki promised them. "I've already eaten one, and I didn't get sick."

The Miyagis were too hungry to refuse. They fed the children first, and Hideki gave a second can to the adults. They all ate with relief, moaning gratefully.

"I don't understand," Grandmother Miyagi said when she'd finished eating. She had black squares and circles and arrows tattooed on the back of her hands, just like the kind old woman who had tried to help Hideki get rid of Rei's *mabui* in the cave. "You say the American devils were nice to you, but we were told they would kill our babies."

"No," Hideki said. "They're only monsters when they're afraid. Just like the Japanese. All the Japanese and Americans care about is killing each other. You should surrender to the Americans."

"*Surrender?*" Father Miyagi said. "But they'll kill us!"

"Not if you go to them now," Hideki replied. "If you wait until they're fighting, until they've all become monsters, they'll eat you up. Do you understand? If you surrender to them without threatening them, they'll help you."

Hideki's suggestion caused a great deal of discussion, but he was too tired to be a part of it. After eating a bit of a candy bar, he laid his head on the American backpack and went to sleep.

When Hideki woke, the Miyagi family had made a decision.

"We're going to surrender," Mother Miyagi said. Father Miyagi didn't look too happy about it, but there wasn't much to argue about at this point. They had run out of food. They wouldn't have lasted a day or two more if Hideki hadn't come along, and he was out of tin cans.

"Will you take us to the Americans?" Grandfather Miyagi asked Hideki.

It would be going backward a little way for Hideki, but he agreed. He walked with the Miyagis out of the tomb, back out into that awful, rainy darkness, and led them the way he had come. He wasn't moving forward anymore. He had been going back for days now, and now he was going back again. But this time it felt right. Like he was working *toward* something at last.

The American soldiers had made camp for the night. They weren't fighting, but they were wary. Hideki made sure the soldiers could see and hear them coming in the darkness, and soon flashlights were shining in their faces, blinding the poor Miyagis, who hadn't seen daylight in more than two months. The Miyagis had tied a white piece of cloth to a pole, and Father Miyagi waved it frantically. An American who spoke bad

Japanese demanded to know who they were, and Hideki answered back in slow Japanese that they were Okinawan refugees.

The grenade in Hideki's pocket had never felt heavier, more conspicuous. He was sure the Americans would see the bulge and shoot him. But after a tense few minutes of interrogation, the Americans finally lowered their lights and their weapons, and someone came to meet the Miyagis.

Hideki tried to slip away into the darkness, but Mother Miyagi saw him. "Aren't you coming with us?" she asked.

Hideki was tempted. He knew the Americans would give him food. Shoes. A dry place to sleep. They would take him away from the fighting, the death. All this misery, all this suffering, would be over for him.

But not for Kimiko.

"No," Hideki told her. "I have to keep going south, to find my sister. I have to make sure she's safe. She's the only family I have left."

Mother Miyagi suddenly pulled Hideki into a hug. He was old enough these days to grumble through a hug from his own mother. But she was gone now, and it had been so long since he'd felt a warm embrace. Hideki let Mother Miyagi hug him, and he hugged her back.

"*Ichariba choodee,*" she said in Okinawan. It meant, "Now that we've met, we're family."

Hideki nodded.

"Thank you, Hideki," she added, releasing him. "I hope you find your sister."

The American soldiers took the Miyagi family away to safety, and Hideki slipped away, headed south once more in search of Kimiko.

THE TOILET SAUNA

Hideki slogged along the highway with thousands more Okinawans and Japanese. When the crowd reached Shikina, a village just outside Naha, some of the IJA soldiers detoured to a command post cave. Hideki decided to go with them. He was leery of setting foot inside another cave with Japanese soldiers, but he needed something more to eat if he was going to have the energy to find his sister. And the command post would have food.

Just the thought of eating made Hideki's head swim and his knees weaken. Almost all his best memories of food were wrapped up with memories of his family. His little brother, Isamu, slurping long Okinawa soba noodles with him at the lantern festival. His mother dishing out a big bowl of *goya champuru*, a sloppy, delicious mix of bitter goya melon and whatever else was in season, whenever their cousins visited. He and his father eating *rafute*, the brown sugar-glazed pork belly so delicate it fell apart in their fingers. Burning his mouth on deep-fried *sātā andāgi*, a kind of round doughnut ball, at a food stall with Kimiko on their way home from one of her *yuta* house calls.

Hideki began to miss his family more than he did a warm meal. And then his appetite for food was erased completely by the sights and smells that greeted him at the command post.

The post was hot, humid, and stinky. Buckets of human waste festered in the corridors. Bags of fermenting, ruined rice sat in puddles of water on the floor. Soldiers walked around in nothing but their loincloths to battle the heat, and no one here had bathed in months. The command officers took turns sticking their heads up the ventilation shafts, desperate for a breath of fresh air. It was like a toilet mixed with a sauna, and Hideki gagged.

One of the half-naked soldiers spied Hideki and grinned. "Hey, girls," he called. "One of your boyfriends has arrived!"

Boyfriend? Girls? What was he talking about?

And then Hideki saw them: *nurses*. Student nurses, like his sister! They were tending to dozens of injured

Japanese soldiers, all laid out on boards. The Shikina Command Post was also a field hospital!

Hideki rushed over to the nearest nurse, a girl just a year or two older than he was. She was wrapping a dirty brown bandage around a soldier's wounded arm.

"Do you have a nurse here named Kimiko?" Hideki asked her. "She's my sister!"

The girl shook her head. She hadn't heard of a nurse named Kimiko, and neither had any of the other people Hideki asked. The excitement Hideki had felt on seeing nurses ebbed away like the tide, and the oppressive heat and stink returned. It was too much to hope that he'd find his sister in the first place he looked.

"Come out!" someone yelled in broken Japanese through the cave entrance. "Come out with hands up!"

Hideki froze. The Americans were *here*. Right outside the cave. They were calling for everyone to come out and surrender!

"We should do it," Hideki said to a Japanese corporal. "We should all surrender."

The soldier stepped away from Hideki in disgust. "Surrender?" he said. "Never!"

Hideki grimaced. The IJA would never give up a command post without a fight. Which meant they were all going to die.

Hideki grabbed the arm of the first nurse he had

talked to. "Quick! Is there another way out of this cave?" he asked.

"Yes," she told him. "At the back."

"Go, go!" Hideki told her.

"But the patients . . ." the girl said.

At the cave entrance, an American soldier peeked inside, his rifle raised. One of the guards at the door slipped out of the shadows and bayonetted him in the gut, and the American screamed.

"Everybody get out, now!" Hideki yelled, and suddenly the air itself exploded. Liquid, dripping flames came shooting through the entrance of the cave, torching the guards and anyone else within twenty feet. The sauna of the command post became an oven. A handful of grenades came clattering in with the flames, and—*B-BOOM!*—the cave entrance collapsed in an explosion of rock and dirt.

Hideki cried out again for everyone to run, but no one was listening anymore. Everyone was screaming and yelling and stampeding for the back of the cave. Soldiers pushed civilians out of the way, and wounded men on the floor cried out for help as they were trampled. Hideki pushed the nurses ahead of him toward the back of the cave. Something came pouring down the ventilation shafts above, splashing everyone ahead of him. Hideki recognized the smell from the car that had brought the Japanese photographer to his school.

Gasoline. The American monsters were pouring gasoline down the ventilation shafts.

A box full of grenades clattered down through the holes, and Hideki knew what came next. He grabbed an empty metal cabinet that stood against the wall and pulled it down on top of himself and the nearest nurse. The cabinet had just banged down on top of them when—*KATHOOM!*—the command post became an inferno.

The explosion of the grenades touched off the ammunition the Japanese army had stored in the cave. The ground beneath Hideki and the nurse rocked like an earthquake. But the metal cabinet stayed on top of them, protecting them from the worst of it. *Fwoosh.* The nurse next to Hideki screamed, and it was only minutes later that Hideki realized he was screaming too. Through their shrieking, they could hear the metal of the cabinet popping as it twisted and warped in the heat. Hideki and the nurse huddled closer as the heat bore down on them. Hideki's bare foot touched the metal cabinet, and it burned against his skin like a wood stove.

With a start, Hideki remembered the grenade in his pocket. How insulated was a ceramic grenade? Would the intense heat set it off? What if he and the nurse had found a safe place in the fiery cave only for his grenade to blow them both to pieces? But there was no place he could throw the grenade now without lifting the cabinet and exposing them to the flames. Hideki curled himself tight around the grenade instead, hoping to shield the nurse from the blast if it went off.

After what seemed like years, the roar of the fire outside died away, and Hideki and the nurse stopped screaming. Hideki's throat was ragged and tight, and his whole body still shook with fear, but he was *alive*. He put a hand to the cabinet wall. It was hot to the touch. He lifted the cabinet with his back instead, putting Rei's backpack between him and the hot metal.

No one had survived except Hideki and the girl. The bodies of nurses and soldiers lay all around them. The girl retched at the sight. Hideki didn't.

Heaven help me, Hideki thought. *I've gotten used to it.*

Hideki took the girl by the hand and ran as quick as he could for the exit at the back of the cave.

FIRE

The girl's name was Masako. She had been a student at a girls' high school in Naha before she and her classmates were conscripted as nurses for the Shikina field hospital.

"It was terrible," she told Hideki as they picked their way slowly up a muddy slope in the darkness. They were only going a few hundred yards, to another command post nearby that Masako knew had nurses. But they had waited until night, when it was safer. Masako had decided to come along with Hideki because she had nowhere else to go.

"At first, it was just scrapes and bruises," Masako said. "But as the Americans pushed south, we received more and more wounded. We ran out of medicine within the first few weeks. Bandages too. We reused those when we could. It was the nurses' job to wash the bandages out in the river while American bombs fell all around us. The only other thing we could do was hold the wounded soldiers' hands and talk to them while they died."

So that was what his sister had been doing the whole time too, Hideki thought. If she was still alive.

Any hope he had to find Kimiko at the next command post was dashed when he and Masako crept through the entrance. It had already been abandoned by the IJA.

Hideki and Masako split up to search the cave for anything to eat or drink. Hideki took a narrow tunnel away from the main passage and came to a small observation room cut into the side of the hill. He stopped to look through the opening and gasped at what he could see in the distance.

Shuri Castle was on fire.

The whole hill was a bright red bonfire in the darkness. The castle's pillars toppled as its ancient walls collapsed in flame.

Hideki was numb as he watched Shuri Castle burn. Of course it was on fire. Of course it was destroyed. He'd been a fool to think the Japanese army could defend Okinawa, and a fool to think that Shuri Castle would survive. Everything on Okinawa would burn. A Divine Wind might still come to save Japan, but no kamikaze was coming to save *this* island. Shuri Castle was gone, and Okinawa was gone with it.

"Hideki! Look! Food!" Masako cried.

Hideki's growling stomach won out over his heartache, and he rushed back to the main cavern. Masako had found a half-empty crate of IJA rations. Food in tin cans. Hideki and Masako had to use bayonets that had been left behind to punch holes in the cans, but it was worth the effort—the tins were filled with delicious pineapple slices. Hideki gulped down two whole cans, making sure to drink every last drop of the sweet pineapple juice.

He was just getting to work on his third can of pineapples when a squad of Japanese soldiers from another command post came into the cave searching for leftover supplies. They immediately confiscated all the tin cans Hideki and Masako hadn't opened.

"Why are you here?" a lieutenant demanded.

"We came here from the field hospital," Hideki said. "The Americans attacked and drove us out."

The lieutenant nodded. "Well, it's time for you to both rejoin the army. Come with us."

No! Not again! Hideki just wanted to find his sister, not get pulled back into the war. He looked around for some place to run, to hide, but one of the soldiers was already grabbing him and Masako by the arms and dragging them to their feet.

"This is your island, after all, not ours," the lieutenant said. "You should be the ones fighting for it."

What island? Hideki thought. What was there left to fight for? And who should he be fighting? Hideki hated the Americans for attacking it, and the Japanese for giving them a reason to attack.

The Japanese soldiers dragged Hideki and Masako to another cave. It wasn't far away, but it hadn't yet been discovered by the Americans. This bunker was crammed full of Japanese soldiers, both healthy and wounded, and eight Okinawan children who had taken refuge with them. Hideki and Masako were quickly forgotten, and the food they had found was taken away and given to the soldiers. Hideki fumed, but didn't say anything. He knew better than to argue.

"We've got to find a way out of here," Hideki told Masako.

"Why?" Masako asked. "Isn't it safer with the soldiers?"

"It wasn't very safe in the field hospital, was it?" Hideki pointed out.

"No, you idiot."

It wasn't Masako who had spoken. It was another girl nearby, a nurse, scolding one of the children. Hideki couldn't see who the girl was, but there was something about the way she said the word *idiot*, something in the scolding yet compassionate tone that made his heart skip a beat. His eyes went wide. Could it be?

Hideki broke away from Masako and flew across the room. Two Japanese soldiers barked at him for squeezing between them, and he almost fell pushing his way through a knot of arguing children, but at last he found her. The nurse had her back to him, tending to a young boy's scraped knee, and Hideki grabbed her by the shoulder and spun her around.

It was Kimiko!

THE GIRL WHO DIED

***"Hideki?"* Kimiko gasped, her eyes growing huge.**

"Kimiko!" Hideki cried.

Hideki couldn't believe his good fortune. His sister was alive, and he'd found her! After all he'd been through, after all he'd done and all he'd lost, finding Kimiko felt like the sun emerging after weeks of rain, and he basked in its warmth.

Hideki hugged his sister tight. After a long minute, Kimiko held Hideki at arm's length and gazed at him like they hadn't seen each other in years. Hideki wondered what he must look like: stick-thin, barefoot, hair a wet, tangled mess, wearing an oversized Japanese uniform. Did he look years older, the way Yoshio had? Kimiko definitely looked older. More adult. Her round face had lengthened, and her full cheeks had flattened.

She looked weary and wary, like she had seen too much to be shocked by anything anymore. Wiser too.

Kimiko wore her nurse's uniform: a gray Western-style pleated dress with short sleeves and a wide white sailor collar. Pouches for bandages and medicine hung from a wide black fabric belt worn high above her waist, and a white nurse's hat covered most of her black hair. Just a hint of the white streak still showed.

Kimiko looked as happy to see Hideki as he felt, but then her face fell and she smacked him hard on the head.

"You idiot," Kimiko told him. "You got here just in time to die with the rest of us."

"Ow! Don't! I hurt my head!" Hideki cried.

Kimiko felt gently in his hair for the wound and found his stitches. "What did you do?" she asked.

"What do you mean die with the rest of you?" Hideki asked, deliberately ignoring her question.

"The Japanese soldiers here are going to attack the Americans tomorrow morning, and we're the first wave," Kimiko told him. "They're going to use the Okinawan children as human shields."

Hideki's heart cracked into pieces and fell apart. He sat down on an empty ammunition box and stared at the boys and girls at the back of the cave. They were all much younger than him, around five to ten years old. They couldn't know what was coming and couldn't do anything about it if they did. To think about these little boys and girls, after all they had already lost, being thrown to the American guns . . . Hideki closed his eyes and cried without tears.

"What are you even doing here?" Kimiko asked him.

"I came to rescue you," Hideki told her.

"Rescue me? I was about to rescue *myself*! And now I have to rescue my little brother too."

"You don't have to rescue me!" Hideki protested. "I'm rescuing you!"

Kimiko's expression shifted from exasperated to suspicious. She squinted and looked him up and down.

"What?" Hideki said.

Kimiko didn't say anything, but it was clear to Hideki that she could see there was something different about him. Could Kimiko see Rei's *mabui* on him, without Hideki even telling her about it?

There was something else he needed to tell her first.

"Kimiko, Otō is dead. So are Anmā and Isamu."

Kimiko put a hand to the wall of the cave to steady herself. "I knew that Anmā and Isamu were gone. I heard their ship had been sunk. But Otō . . . I sensed he had gone to join our ancestors, but I didn't know for sure." Tears spilled from her eyes. "You and I are all that's left now."

"That's why I came for you," Hideki told her. "I was with Otō when he died. I promised him I would find you, and I did."

Kimiko laid a hand on his shoulder, and Hideki covered his sister's hand with his own.

"I never told our parents what really happened to me. How I got the white streak in my hair," Kimiko said. "I never told anybody."

Hideki frowned. He couldn't remember a time when she *didn't* have the white streak.

"It was years ago, when you were just a baby. I was too little to go in the ocean without Otō or Anmā there, but I did it anyway. Me and Fumiko, another girl from the village. A giant wave came and tumbled me, sweeping me under and flipping me over and over so I didn't know which way was up. I've never felt so helpless, so out of control. I couldn't breathe. Couldn't scream. I hit my head on a rock and passed out, and the next thing I knew I was flat on my back on the sand and Fumiko was bent over me, sobbing. She told me I wasn't breathing when she pulled me out of the water. I had drowned. I was dead, and now I was alive again."

Hideki was aghast. How had he never heard this story before?

"I never told Otō and Anmā what happened, because I didn't want to get into trouble. But when my hair grew back in the place where I'd cut myself, it grew in white. And from that day on I had a special connection with the dead. That's why I'm a *yuta.*" Her voice grew soft. “I’ve been dead once, Hideki, and I don’t want to die again.”

“Then we’ve got to get out of here,” said Hideki. “Is there another way out of the cave?”

“Yes,” Kimiko told him. “But you’re not going to like it.”

THE MOTHER OF ALL BOMBS

Kimiko was right. Hideki didn't like it.

An unexploded bomb the size of a cow sat in the mud right in the mouth of the cave's back entrance. The bomb was greenish gray, with four black fins sticking up at the back and a yellow band painted around the base of its nose cone.

Why the huge bomb hadn't gone off when it hit was a mystery, and the slightest touch now might set it off. If it exploded, the whole cave would be blown to bits.

It was the mother of all bombs, and there was barely room to squeeze past it. The IJA hadn't even bothered to leave a guard by this back exit, because they thought no one would be crazy enough to go near the bomb.

Hideki took a step back in fear.

"That's the only way out?" he asked.

"Yes," Kimiko told him. "It's either that, or we die tomorrow with those soldiers. I overheard the generals at the command post. The plan is for the IJA to hold out as long as they can at each ridge. Just when the Americans are about to overrun them, they retreat to the next ridge and start all over again, all the way to the southern end of the island. In between retreats, they send infiltration squads to attack the Americans by night. But they're not meant to survive either. The Japanese army was never going to win, Hideki. They're just here to slow the Americans down. They're trying to take as many American soldiers with them as they can. And as many Okinawans too, I guess."

Hideki felt numb. *One plane for one battleship, one man for ten of the enemy.* Wasn't that what Lieutenant Colonel Sano had told the Blood and Iron Student Corps before sending them out with their grenades to attack the Americans? That night outside his school felt like years ago to Hideki.

But the price of an Okinawan life was far cheaper even than one man for ten of the enemy. Far cheaper than the life of one Japanese soldier, that was for sure. And Hideki was tired of sacrificing people he cared about.

"Then we do it," Hideki said. "The bomb might go off, and it might not. But if we stay, the IJA will definitely kill us, and at least this way we have a chance."

Kimiko looked sideways at Hideki, like she was measuring him again, but she didn't say anything.

Hideki and Kimiko went back to the main part of the cave. They told Masako the plan, and very quietly the three of them gathered the eight Okinawan children and led them to the back entrance.

Masako gasped when she saw the bomb. "We have to get past *that*?"

"You can do it. We have to," Hideki said. He turned to his sister. "You and Masako go out first. I'll send the kids out to you. Get them as far away from the bomb as you can."

Kimiko nodded. She approached the bomb, took a deep breath, and slid sideways between the cave wall and the metal shell. The space was too narrow to avoid touching the bomb, and gently, oh so gently, she put her hands against it. Hideki held his breath, and Masako closed her eyes.

Kimiko wiggled sideways, and the gap between the bomb and the wall got tighter. Tighter. She spread her arms around the bomb and carefully rested her weight against it as she slithered through the narrowest spot . . . and then she was past it and outside. Hideki let out his breath, and beside him, Masako opened her eyes and bit off a sob of relief.

"You're next," Hideki told her.

"I can't do it," she said.

"You can," Hideki told her. "We survived that cave of flames, didn't we? These kids need you to be just as strong as you were for those injured soldiers in the hospital. I know you can do it. Just do what Kimiko did."

Masako took a deep breath and nodded. She avoided the bomb as long as she could, pressing herself against the cave wall, but soon the space grew too narrow. Too short. She froze, her back curled against the cave wall, holding her body just centimeters from the curving side of the bomb. Kimiko called encouragement to her from where she stood outside, but Masako couldn't go any farther. She closed her eyes and shook her head, her trembling body hovering just inches above the bomb.

"Masako, you can do it," Hideki told her again.

"No. No! I've seen what American bombs do to bodies! I don't want to end up like that!" Masako cried.

"You won't," Hideki said. He looked at the frightened children with him. "None of us will."

Masako just shook her head more forcefully. She wasn't going to budge. But she couldn't keep pressing herself into the curving wall at her back forever, and with a scream of panic she lost her balance. With nothing to grab on to, she fell face-first onto the bomb.

Clang!

Hideki gasped and closed his eyes, waiting for the mother of all bombs to explode.

STANDOFF

The bomb didn't explode. Not yet. But Masako was done. Her courage was exhausted. Her legs gave out, and she started to slide to the ground, sobbing. But Kimiko was there on the other side to take her hand and pull her the rest of the way past the bomb, out into the rain.

Hideki sighed with relief, but he still had a job to do. He straightened and addressed the children.

"There, see? They both got past! We can do it too!" Hideki told them. "It's like a game. Who can get through without touching any of the metal?"

The children were wise to him though. If Masako's fear hadn't already infected them, they had all seen enough bombs in the last two months, enough death, to understand the danger. They knew this wasn't a game.

But if Hideki had learned anything from playing with his younger brother, Isamu, it was that little kids were often brave where teenagers and adults were scared. Because little kids thought they were invincible. The number of times Isamu had jumped down from a branch that was too high, or put his hands too close to the kitchen fire, or tried to pet a strange dog . . . Hideki got choked up thinking about his little brother. Isamu, who had been brave enough to leave half his family and board a strange ship for a land he'd never been to before. Isamu, whom he would never see again.

Hideki shook off his sorrow for his little brother, saving it for another time. If he didn't get these children past the mother of all bombs, they would all be joining Isamu too soon.

One by one, Hideki helped the boys and girls slide around the bomb and into Kimiko's waiting hands outside. Hideki's stomach was full of butterflies the whole time, but not because he worried about the bomb going off and killing *him*, he realized. Because he didn't want any more children, any more innocent Okinawans, to die for a fight that wasn't theirs.

"Halt! Where are you going? What are you doing?" someone yelled, and Hideki spun.

A Japanese soldier was aiming a rifle right at them.

"Stop or I'll shoot!" the Japanese soldier cried.

Hideki's heart caught in his throat. His first instinct

was to panic. To run. But there was nowhere to run. And he'd been through too much by now to panic over a nervous IJA private aiming a shaky gun at him. Like Kimiko, Hideki didn't want to die. But he wasn't afraid of death anymore either.

A steadying calm came over Hideki. It stilled him from head to toe like the cool breeze off the sea in summer, and all the tension left him.

Hideki stepped in front of the last of the children, a little boy. Right in between the soldier on one side and the boy and the bomb on the other.

"Go ahead," Hideki said.

The soldier frowned. "What?"

"Go ahead and shoot," Hideki told him. "But just know that if you miss, or if the bullet goes through me, you'll hit the bomb behind me and then you'll be dead too. We all will be."

The soldier's rifle dipped as he realized Hideki was right. Hideki watched the private's eyes dart this way and that as he considered his options.

"What's your name?" Hideki asked the remaining little boy.

"Kazuo," he squeaked.

"Go on, Kazuo. You'll be all right," Hideki told him.

The Japanese soldier took aim with his rifle again. "No one is allowed to leave! Come away from there at once or I'll shoot!"

The little boy looked to Hideki for direction, and Hideki nodded for him to go on past the bomb.

"Stop!" the soldier said. He raised his rifle again, but Kazuo didn't stop and the soldier didn't shoot. When Kazuo was safely through, Hideki slid the pack off his shoulders and turned to leave.

"I said stop!" the soldier cried. There was panic in his voice. A panic Hideki no longer felt.

Hideki handed his backpack through the narrow gap to Kimiko, then slid sideways to follow it. If the soldier tried to shoot him now, he had a better chance of hitting the bomb than Hideki.

"No one is permitted to leave!" the private yelled.

A riptide pulled at Hideki's stomach as the distance between the wall and the bomb got narrower and narrower. He was going to have to put his hands on the thing, wrap his arms around it the way everyone else had. Would his touching the bomb now set it off at last? Would the soldier let his orders override his common sense? Had Kimiko and Masako gotten the children far enough away where they wouldn't be hurt?

Distracted by his own thoughts and fears, Hideki lost his balance the way Masako had. He'd meant to let himself against the bomb slowly, gently, but now he fell onto it with a teeth-rattling *thud*.

Clang! The ceramic grenade in Hideki's pocket whacked the side of the bomb like a hammer, and he flinched and closed his eyes. Had the grenade cracked? Was it going to explode?

Hideki froze for what seemed like an eternity, wondering if he was dead and just didn't know it. At last he took a deep breath and opened his eyes. Gray-painted metal and lines of rivets stared back at him. Water streamed down the side of the bomb like the sweat running down Hideki's back. The bomb was still there, and so was he.

Hideki glanced sideways to see what the soldier was doing, but he was gone.

"Hideki! Come on!" Kimiko called to him. He turned to look the other way, and there she was, right by the bomb. She hadn't run off and left him.

Hideki closed his eyes and slithered the rest of the way around the bomb, the grenade in his pocket digging into him as it scraped along. And then it wasn't scraping anymore, and there was more room between the cave wall and Hideki, and Kimiko was taking his hand and pulling him free.

Hideki fell into his sister's waiting arms, and she held him while he shook. All the tension of the moment washed back over him. He and Kimiko hadn't hugged like this in a long time. They were both too old for that kind of thing. But now neither of them cared. They were still alive, and they were together, and they held on to each other like they would never let go again.

"What is that?" Kimiko said at last, feeling the hard lump in Hideki's shirt pocket.

"A grenade," Hideki said. He pulled it out and showed it to her.

"That's not a grenade, you idiot," Kimiko said. "It's a piece of pottery."

"It is too a grenade," Hideki said. "And it works. I know." That was all he said. Kimiko seemed to understand there was more to the story, but she let it go. For now.

"*You have a grenade?*" Masako called. She was watching them from beyond the next hill, where she waited with the children. "Use it on the bomb!"

"What?" Hideki said. "Why?"

"To close the cave off. To blow them all up!" Masako called. She knelt and put her arms around a little boy, the one who had still been in the cave when the Japanese soldier threatened to shoot them. "It's only fair, after what they were going to do to us!"

Hideki thought about it as he and Kimiko joined the others. At last he shook his head and put the grenade back in his pocket.

"You told me to be brave enough to slide past that beast, but you're not brave enough to throw your grenade at it?" Masako challenged him.

Hideki frowned. Was he just being a coward again? Maybe. But there was more to it than that. He couldn't explain it to Masako. He wasn't even sure he could explain it to himself.

Shouts came from inside the cave. The soldier had gone back for help! Hideki didn't know if any of them would be able to squeeze past the bomb, or would set it off trying, but he didn't want to be around to find out.

"Come on," he told the others. "Time to go!"

"Where?" Kimiko asked him. "South?"

"No," Hideki told her. "North. Back through the front lines. We're going home."

LIES AND DREAMS

Hideki led Kimiko, Masako, and the children on a zigzag path up muddy hills and down blasted valleys. But always north. Toward the illumination shells and the gunshots and explosions.

Toward home.

Hideki, Kimiko, and Masako pulled the last of the children up to the top of a steep ridge. They stopped to take a breather, but something about this particular place made Hideki's skin prickle. He motioned for the others to be quiet and stay where they were, and he crept down the other side of the ridge, holding on to tree stumps so as not to slide.

And there it was. A Japanese army machine gun nest. It was pointed north, toward the direction the advancing Americans would come from. Hideki was standing on the hill above the nest, where the Japanese soldiers inside couldn't see him. But they *would* see Hideki and others when they passed by, and the soldiers would likely shoot them as spies, or for running away.

Hideki snuck back to report his findings to Kimiko and Masako.

"Why can't we just go around them?" Kimiko asked. "Head west for a while, then turn back north?"

Hideki shook his head. "If there's a nest here, then there are nests up and down this ridgeline, to the west and east. This is the new defensive line. If we don't find a way past this machine gun, we'll just have to find a way past the next one."

"What do we do?" Masako asked.

"I'll take care of it," Hideki said. "Give me five minutes, then take the kids over the ridge and down through the next valley. I'll keep the machine gunners distracted."

"How?" Kimiko asked.

Hideki shrugged and headed back down the ridge. "I'll think of something."

"Use your grenade," Masako hissed.

Hideki considered it again. His last grenade. The one the IJA had given him to kill himself with. The fragile ceramic thing had survived the whole awful battle. All he had to do was chuck the thing through the hole cut in the hillside, and the machine gun nest would be destroyed. So would the soldiers who operated it. Then Kimiko and Masako and the children could slip safely by.

Hideki thought he saw something moving out of the corner of his eye, and he glanced sideways at it. But no one was there. Hideki put a hand to the stitches under his hair and wondered if he was sensing the ghost of Rei, or if his head wound was playing tricks on him. Either way, it was a stark reminder of what happened when you threw grenades at people.

He would just have to find a different way to distract the soldiers.

Hideki returned to the hill above the machine gun nest and took a deep breath. He had to make this work. For Kimiko. And Masako. And the little kids.

"*Yōkai,*" Hideki said, loud enough for the soldiers inside to hear him.

"What?" someone called from the bunker. "Who said that? Who's there?"

"*Yōkai!*" Hideki said again.

"You don't sound like a ghost!" the soldier called back. He still couldn't see who was talking, and Hideki could hear the rising panic in the soldier's voice.

"*Yōkai* is the new password," Hideki said. "I'm from headquarters. You're supposed to give me the response."

"Response? We don't know the response!" the soldier called back. "Nobody tells us anything out here!"

"All right, all right," Hideki said. "I can tell you're Japanese. I'm coming down."

Hideki scrambled down the muddy slope and climbed inside the tiny machine gun nest. There were only two soldiers there, both Japanese army privates. Their clothes were muddy and oversized, like the men had shrunk in the rain, and they each had scraggly beards that showed just how long they'd been alone. The bunker reeked of sweat and urine, and there were three inches of water on the floor. Between them stood a Type 92 Heavy Machine Gun.

How long had Hideki been gone? Was it already five minutes? He had to hurry. Kimiko and Masako and the kids might already be moving by now.

"Private Hideki Kaneshiro, Blood and Iron Student Corps," Hideki said, saluting them. "Lieutenant Colonel Sano sent me." It wasn't exactly a lie.

Through the window of the bunker, Hideki caught a flash of movement. It wasn't Rei's ghost this time—it was Kimiko, Masako, and the kids. They were out in the open, where the machine gunners could see them if they looked. Hideki slid around to the back side of the cave so the soldiers had to turn away from them to see him.

"What's the message?" one of the soldiers asked.

"Yes! The message," Hideki said. He hadn't thought that far ahead yet. Ideas swarmed in his mind like flies, but none of them landed. Behind the soldiers, one of the children slipped in the mud and fell, and Kimiko stopped to help him up.

"The *Yamato*," Hideki said. "The big battleship is coming to save us!"

"What? We heard it was sunk!" one of the soldiers said.

"No! That was just a rumor started by the high command to fool the Americans. The *Yamato* is still floating and will soon chase the American armada away so more reinforcements can land!"

It might have been a tall tale, but it was one the two soldiers desperately wanted to believe. They laughed and clapped each other on the shoulders. As life came back into their faces, Hideki saw how young they were under those beards. Barely older than he was.

Behind the soldiers, Kimiko and the others were still visible, climbing a long, low hill.

"Where are you from?" Hideki asked, trying to stall for time.

"Hiroshima," one of the boys said. "I was going to go to university to study chemistry, but then I was drafted into the army."

"I'm from Iwaki," the other boy said. "My father and I were fishermen before the navy confiscated our boat. Then he and I were both drafted. He's in Korea now."

The two soldiers were quiet for a moment, remembering the people they used to be. *Their lives got interrupted by the war just like mine*, Hideki realized. It was easy to think of the soldiers as the ones doing the interrupting. As the people who had come to disrupt the peace of Okinawa. But neither of these boys had volunteered for this. They both had things they'd been doing, families they longed to see again, plans for the future. All that had been taken away from them too.

"Do you have any food in that pack, Private?" one of the soldiers asked.

Hideki's heart fluttered at the offer of a perfect new distraction—until he remembered he and the others had already eaten everything he had.

"I'm sorry, I don't have food," he told them. "But I do have cigarettes!"

The look on the soldiers' faces told Hideki he was their new best friend. Hideki took his time emptying his pack to look for the cigarettes and stole a quick glance outside. Kimiko helped the last of the children over the hill, and they disappeared into the darkness. Hideki smiled with relief, and relaxed. He didn't have to keep the soldiers' attention any longer, and his thoughts turned to how quickly now he could get away and rejoin Kimiko.

"What's this?" one of the soldiers asked.

Hideki had taken the oilskin pouch of photographs out to find the cigarettes, and one of the soldiers had picked it up and was looking inside.

"Oh. That's . . . pictures," Hideki said, though the soldiers could clearly see that's what they were. *Pictures of dead soldiers and their families*, he thought, but he couldn't say that.

The soldiers lit cigarettes and flipped through the pictures, studying the faces and places. With each image of their long-lost home, the mood in the bunker became more and more melancholy.

"Why do you have all these?" one of the soldiers asked.

Hideki couldn't explain *mabui*. Couldn't explain Rei. Not here. Not now. He said instead, "The American ones were in a pack I took from a soldier after he was dead. After I killed him. The others . . . soldiers gave to me for safekeeping."

The soldiers might have understood that the men who "gave" Hideki the photos were all dead now, but they accepted the little white lie. The two young men smoked their cigarettes and thought of home, and Hideki sat awkwardly, itching to get his pictures back and leave.

"I should get back to headquarters," Hideki said at last.

The soldiers nodded and handed him back the pictures.

"Hey, can I give you a picture too?" one of them said. He pulled a wrinkled, water-stained photo from his jacket pocket. He hesitated, reluctant to let it go, then handed it to Hideki. "It's me and my mother, back in Iwaki," he said. "For safekeeping, like the others. You know, in case the *Yamato* doesn't come in time for us."

"Me too," the other soldier said. He gave Hideki a picture of him and his sweetheart, a pretty young woman who lived in Hiroshima.

They knew, Hideki realized. They knew the *Yamato* was a lie. If not his lie, then somebody else's. That the dream of victory was just that—a dream. The reality was, they were all going to die here on Okinawa. And soon.

And Hideki and his sister and the children were going to die with them if they couldn't get past the American army next.

LION-DOGS

Hideki hadn't walked too far when he found Kimiko, Masako, and the children all hiding behind an exploded Japanese truck. To their left, Hideki could hear the roar of the sea. To their right, a steep rock cliff rose like teeth from the ground.

"Sorry you had to wait for me," Hideki said.

"We didn't have a choice," Masako said. She nodded for Hideki to follow her, and together the two of them crawled through the mud to a bend in the road. Just beyond them was an American camp. Someone—either the Americans or the Japanese before them—had cut down trees so that they fell across the road, and the soldiers guarding the camp stood behind the log barricade, facing south. Behind them, Hideki could see other soldiers at a cookfire they'd sheltered from the rain.

Hideki made a frame with his fingers. There were at least ten American soldiers, including two guards so close Hideki could hit them with a rock.

Or a grenade.

The American camp couldn't have been more than a few dozen meters from the Japanese machine gun nest Hideki had just left. It was almost dawn, and as soon as the sun rose, these American soldiers would advance south and run right into the young Japanese soldiers. They would fight, and the Americans would win—they always won, eventually—but in the meantime, Hideki and the others would be caught in the cross fire.

They had to get past the Americans before that happened.

Hideki nodded for Masako to turn around, and together they returned to where Kimiko and the children waited.

"Well?" Kimiko asked.

"The Americans are taking up the whole road," Hideki explained. "There's no way to sneak by without them seeing us."

"What if we went out in the water and swam around them?" Kimiko suggested.

Hideki shook his head. "If they see us in the water, they'll think we're a Japanese attack force and start shooting at us."

"Do you still have that grenade?" Masako asked.

"Yes," Hideki said. "But I can't kill them all with one grenade. There's too many of them."

"We don't have to kill them all," Masako said. "Just a few of them. We throw it from the ocean side, to make them think the Japanese army is attacking from the beach. While they're shooting at shadows, we run behind them, along the road. Then we're safe!"

Hideki pulled the grenade out of his pocket, weighing it in his hand as he walked off by himself. Masako's plan was dangerous, but it could work. He'd seen the Americans when they were angry. They were like *shisa*. Lion-dogs. When they got something in their teeth, they shook it until it was dead. They would destroy the beach with machine guns and mortars and grenades, and then go down there with rifles and bayonets to make sure there wasn't anyone left. That's when Hideki and the others could slip on by.

Kimiko joined Hideki, leaving Masako with the children.

"What are you thinking, Hideki?" his sister asked him quietly.

Hideki tried to put it into words, the way he hadn't been able to when Masako wanted him to use his grenade on the mother of all bombs. The way he'd felt when he decided not to use his grenade on the Japanese soldiers in the machine gun nest.

"I'm thinking . . . that this isn't our fight," Hideki

told her. "It's not between Okinawa and America, or Okinawa and Japan. It's between America and Japan. Why can't we just let them duke it out?"

"Because Okinawa is caught in the middle, just like we are," Kimiko said.

"All this time, people kept telling me, 'This is your island, you should be defending it,'" Hideki said. "But I wasn't defending it. I was fighting for somebody else's side while they both destroyed my home. And I'm tired of it. I want to be on Okinawa's side for once."

"So use the grenade on the Americans to save some Okinawans," Kimiko told him.

Kimiko had a point. If he used the grenade here and now, he could lead them all to safety. Masako. The children. *Kimiko.* That's what he'd really promised his father after all, wasn't it? Not just to find his sister, but to keep what was left of his family together. To *live.* And sometimes you had to fight to live. Maybe he needed to fight to save Okinawa too.

The thought of fighting made Hideki remember all the awful things he'd seen each side do to each other, the awful things *both* sides had done to Okinawans in the name of war.

"No," Hideki said. "No, if we attack them, we're their enemy. When they're not under attack, when they're not afraid, the Americans are human beings. They actually helped me. Gave me medicine. Sewed up my head.

It's the same with the Japanese. The photographer, my principal, my teachers, they were nice to me before the Americans came. That machine gun nest back there, it didn't have two monsters in it. It had two human beings. But if I threw this grenade at them, they would have turned into monsters. Just like these Americans. They'll become monsters that breathe fire and bullets. They're not at war with Okinawa. They're at war with Japan. But if I throw this grenade at them, they'll be at war with Okinawa too."

"Okinawa *is* Japan," Kimiko said.

"Are we?" Hideki asked.

Kimiko was quiet for a time, then said, "We have to do *something*, Hideki."

Hideki stared at the grenade in his hand. If he didn't use his last grenade here and now, when would he ever use it?

And that's when he knew what he had to do.

NAKED

To the east, the black night sky was beginning to turn blue over the high, jagged ridge. "It's almost dawn," Hideki said. "As soon as the sun's up, we'll surrender."

"*Surrender?*" Masako said. She'd come to see what he and Kimiko were talking about. "We can't surrender to the Americans! They'll kill us!"

"Not if we don't make them afraid," Hideki said. He remembered the HOW TO SURRENDER leaflets that had fallen on him the day after the Americans had first landed. How long ago that seemed now! What had the papers said? Stay away from the Japanese army. Wear white. Make it clear you were surrendering, and not a threat.

He also remembered the Japanese using Okinawans as human shields, and how the Americans had gunned down Okinawans who were no threat at all because they were afraid there were explosives or Japanese soldiers hidden under their kimonos.

Hideki and the others didn't have anything white to wear—all their clothes were muddy brown. So how would they convince the Americans they were harmless?

Hideki had felt powerless many times in his life, especially since the Americans had landed. But one moment stood out among them all. Hideki remembered being naked on the battlefield, shivering in the rain as he peeled layer after layer of maggot-filled, bloody clothes off his body. Stripped down until there was nothing left of him. A ghost. He'd felt so exposed. So unprotected. It was horrifying.

That was how they had to be now if they wanted to survive.

"We'll go naked," Hideki said.

"*What?*" Masako said.

"It's the only way," Hideki told them. "At least down to our underclothes. We have to be as harmless as possible. As long as we don't make them scared, we'll be all right. But if anybody does anything to make them angry, or afraid . . ."

Hideki didn't have to tell them what they would do if that happened.

"Hideki, are you sure about this?" Kimiko asked him.

The sky behind the sawtooth ridge to the east turned orange. The sun was almost up.

"Tell the kids to take their clothes off," Hideki said. "It's time."

Hideki stepped away from the others and pulled off Rei's pack. The only thing he took out from it was the oilskin envelope with the photographs. Hideki removed his Japanese army jacket and pants and slid the waterproof pouch down the back of his underpants, the only piece of clothing he still wore.

Hideki put his helmet upside down in the mud, then folded his clothes and nestled them neatly inside it. On the very top, he placed his grenade. The one the IJA had given him to kill himself with. Hideki had finally understood: *This* is what he had to do with his last grenade. If he took it with him now, it *would* kill him.

To live, Hideki had to leave his only weapon behind.

SURRENDER

Hideki felt like he was about to brave the Gauntlet back at school, but this gauntlet was deadly serious. How had he ever been afraid of Yoshio and his friends when there were things that were far scarier in the world?

The sun was just over the crest of the ridge when Hideki, Kimiko, and Masako walked around the bend, followed by eight small children. All of them wore nothing but their underclothes. For Hideki and the other boys, that meant once-white, now-gray shorts. The girls wore gray underpants, with another piece of gray cloth tied tight around the chest for Kimiko and Masako. The younger children were more comfortable with their nakedness, but Hideki knew how Kimiko and Masako and the older children must be feeling. Defenseless. Exposed. Vulnerable.

Hopefully, the Americans would see them the same way.

The soldiers stood behind the barricade of fallen trees. Hideki and the others had just come within sight of the first American sentries when the clouds above them parted, and for the first time in a solid month, the rain stopped. It was like someone had suddenly dammed up a river.

Hideki stopped and blinked as actual sunlight came streaming through, warm on his naked skin. The children all stopped in their tracks, forgetting for a moment they were walking into a viper's nest. It distracted the soldiers on guard too. For a long moment, everyone on the road and in the camp stopped and looked up at the sun, like none of them had ever imagined living to see it again.

And then one of the soldiers cried out and pointed at the children, and the moment was broken.

The two guards at the perimeter of the camp aimed their rifles at them and shouted things Hideki didn't understand. Hideki's hand instinctively went for his grenade, but of course it wasn't there. He felt a twinge of panic at leaving his only protection behind. But no—if he had a grenade in his hand right now, he would already be dead.

Within seconds, more soldiers had run to take up positions behind the fallen logs that ringed their camp.

An entire squad pointed their guns straight at Hideki and the others. One of the smaller boys whimpered and tried to turn around, but Kimiko took his hand and comforted him.

Hideki took a step forward, and the American soldiers erupted with unintelligible, angry shouts. Hideki's heart beat so hard he thought it would bust out of his chest. What had he done? How would they survive this? If the American soldiers fired at them now, they were helpless. They would all be dead. They didn't even speak the same language.

One of the soldiers barked at them again in English, but no one understood it.

Hideki took another step forward.

The Americans shouted again, and they squinted down the barrels of their rifles. Hideki could just imagine their fingers tightening around the triggers. Squeezing . . .

This wasn't going at all like it had when he'd surrendered with the Miyagi family. The Americans were too on edge now. The sunlight had startled everyone. Made it look like Hideki and the others had appeared out of nowhere. Hideki felt a bead of sweat trickle down his forehead and hit his bare chest. Beside him, one of the little girls started to cry.

"It's going to be all right," Hideki told the children with a courage he didn't feel.

One of the soldiers barked louder than all the others, and Hideki trembled as the biggest man he'd ever seen pushed his way to the front of the soldiers. He was more bear than man, and he carried a big rifle that was as long as Hideki was tall. His face was dark with stubble, and Hideki realized with a start that one of his ears was completely gone, replaced by a scarred red crater the size and shape of a coconut crab. Hideki fought the urge to take a step back, and he stood his ground.

"Do not move," the big bear-man said. The intonation was all wrong, but Hideki thought he understood it. The American was speaking Japanese.

Hideki glanced around Masako and his sister, and they shared in his amazement and relief. Quickly, Kimiko and Masako made sure the children understood.

"Okay. Okay," Hideki said, repeating something he'd heard the Americans say at the field hospital where he was treated.

"Do not be tricks," the bear-man said.

"We surrender!" Hideki said, hoping the bear-man understood. He pronounced the Japanese word more slowly: "Sur-ren-der."

The big bear-man glanced around at the other soldiers, and they grunted slowly at each other. Hideki guessed they were debating what he had said.

Hideki turned his palms up to show them he wasn't carrying a weapon and took a step forward.

"*Woh, woh, woh!*" the soldiers yelled, and the rifles that had dipped came clacking back up at him.

"Don't shoot!" Hideki pleaded. "Don't shoot!"

"*Raise you hands!*" the bear-man growled. "*Obey or I fire!*"

Hideki quickly put his hands up and urged the others to do the same. All around him, Kimiko, Masako, and the children did as they were told and threw their hands up as high as they could go. There. There was no way the Americans could see them as a threat now. They were naked. Weaponless. Obedient.

PA-KOW!

A single shot rang out, the sound booming off the steep ridge wall to their right, and Hideki flinched.

Before the last echo had faded away, the little boy beside him, Kazuo, the one who'd been the last to squeeze through past the bomb before Hideki, the one he'd guarded with his life, fell face forward into the mud.

RISE UP

The children screamed. Kimiko cried out. Hideki dropped into the mud next to the boy, his hands over his head, and the others did the same.

"Kazuo! Kazuo, are you all right?" Hideki shouted.

Kazuo cried in pain, but he was alive. He was alive, but the Americans had shot him. Tears sprang to Hideki's eyes.

We're all going to die, he thought. *They shot Kazuo, and we're all going to die.* He wanted to get up and check on Kazuo, but he was too afraid of being shot. He kept his face down in the mud.

"We did what they told us!" Kimiko cried. "We did exactly what they told us to do, and they still shot at us!"

She didn't understand, but Hideki did. He knew

now why otherwise normal men became monsters. It wasn't just when you threatened them. They became monsters when they were *afraid*. It didn't excuse it, but it explained it. These men had been pushed past the edge of fear. The Battle of Okinawa had done it to Japanese soldiers, to American soldiers—even to Hideki himself. He had hoped to slip past the front lines when things were calm enough for both sides to be human, but he realized now that was impossible. It was too late.

They were all monsters now.

Hideki squeezed his eyes shut tight and waited for more bullets.

But they didn't come. What he heard instead was more shouting among the Americans. He looked up to see the big bear of a man grabbing the rifle of a smaller, younger soldier and twisting it toward the sky. The bear-man roared at the young soldier, then at the other soldiers. He was angry. The young soldier must have been the one who shot the boy, and the big bear was mad at him.

More soldiers shouted and argued, but the big bear-man had the last word. The Americans kept their rifles trained on Hideki and the others, but they were more sheepish now. They didn't bark and snap at them like dogs. Didn't squint down their rifle barrels like they were about to shoot.

Hideki took a deep breath. He had to get help for

Kazuo. And he and Kimiko and Masako and the others all had to get moving if they wanted to live. That shot had echoed far and wide in the early morning stillness. The Japanese soldiers had to have heard it. An infiltration squad could be here any moment, and then nothing the bear-man said or did would save them. Hideki and the others would be caught in the middle of a gun fight.

Slowly, fearfully, Hideki pushed himself up out of the mud and stood.

"Hideki! What are you doing?" Kimiko cried.

Naked, shivering, covered with mud, Hideki put his hands in the air again and stared at the big soldier. This was it. Neither of them needed to speak the same language to understand. There were only two ways this could end. Either he let Hideki and the others go by, or he killed them where they stood.

A long moment passed between them, and then the bear-man said something in English that sounded quiet and gentle. Apologetic. He lowered his enormous rifle and nodded.

Legs shaking, Hideki walked slowly, carefully, over to Kazuo and gently lifted him out of the mud. Kazuo had been shot through the arm. There was blood, and the arm was limp like it was broken, but Kazuo would live if Hideki could get him to one of the American doctors. Kazuo buried his head in Hideki's chest, sobbing quietly.

"It's going to be okay, Kazuo," Hideki whispered. "I'll protect you."

Hideki knew he couldn't really protect Kazuo from being shot. He couldn't protect *any* of them from being shot. But he would try, at least. And he would die trying, if he had to.

"Get the little ones on their feet," Hideki told Kimiko. She stood, warily, borrowing some of Hideki's bravery. "Come on, Masako. You too," Hideki said.

Masako didn't stand up. "They shot him," she said, staring at Kazuo's injured arm. "They'll shoot us too."

"They might," Hideki said. "But there's nothing else we can do."

Kimiko helped Masako up and held her hand. Kimiko took one of the children's hands as well. One by one they took each other's hands, the last of the children clutching Hideki's arm so hard it started to go numb, forming a ten-person-long chain across the road.

And then they began to walk.

American soldiers still pointed guns at them, and one or two of the little kids backed up a step, still afraid of what these strangers might do.

"Don't run," Hideki told the children. "Keep your eyes down. Don't do anything to make them think you're a threat."

They drew closer and closer to the Americans. To the barrels of the guns. The big bear-man said something that carried a warning tone, and Hideki glanced up. But the bear-man wasn't talking to the children. He was admonishing the other soldiers. Was he telling them not to shoot? A couple of them gave him angry, skeptical looks, but the bear-man appeared to be the boss.

Hideki put his eyes on the ground again. "We're almost there," he told the children. "Be brave and just keep walking."

Kazuo had gone limp in his arms. Either from exhaustion or shock, Hideki didn't know, but Kazuo had passed out. It was just as well. Seeing the soldiers with their guns, knowing what they could do, made Hideki's whole body quiver with fear.

They were almost there. Almost there . . .

Hideki's bare foot passed through a gap in the barricades, and he was across the line. Masako and Kimiko and the children had made it too. Hideki's breath left him and he collapsed to his knees, sobbing. They had done it. They were through. They were safe. Hideki looked up at the big bear-man with relief and gratitude, and hoped he understood.

And then the Japanese army found them.

OVER THE LINE

A Japanese machine gun blared behind them— *chu-chu-chu-chu-chu!*—and one of the American soldiers right in front of Hideki went down. There were screams, shouts, and then Americans were shooting back. The big bear-man's rifle boomed right over Hideki's head.

Chu-chu-chung! Chu-chu-chu-chu-chung!

Hideki ducked behind one of the logs in the road, shielding Kazuo with his body. His sister and Masako and all the other children dove for cover too. They were safe from the firestorm. From the monsters at each other's throats.

Bullets tore into the trees at their backs, and a grenade exploded a few yards beyond them, in the heart of the American camp. Hideki threw his hands over his head and prayed to his ancestors to see him safely through. Beside him, the big bear-man dropped down to reload his enormous rifle and pull out a grenade of his own.

"Rei?" the big soldier said, and Hideki looked up. The bear-man with the missing ear was looking around like there was somebody else there whom neither of them could see.

Hideki knew that feeling all too well.

The big soldier looked down at Hideki and frowned. Did he recognize Rei's *mabui* on Hideki? Could he?

The big soldier shook off whatever it was he was feeling, pulled the pin on his grenade, and stood to throw it.

Another American soldier hurried up to Hideki. This soldier had no weapon and was wearing a white armband with a red cross on it. Hideki recognized the armband as the same one the doctors at the camp had worn, and he gratefully handed off Kazuo to the man. Then Hideki followed along, crouching as he ran. Behind him, more soldiers with red crosses on their armbands pulled Kimiko and Masako and the other children away.

Bullets still flew and grenades still exploded, but Hideki wasn't afraid anymore. He knew they would be all right now. In the camps away from the battlefield, the Americans would be human again, and Hideki and

Kimiko and all the other Okinawan children would get the food and water and medical attention they required.

There was only one thing Hideki still needed, but for that, the Americans couldn't help him.

For that, he needed a *yuta*.

A BEGINNING

Hideki and Kimiko slipped away from the American refugee camp and climbed the hill up to what was left of Shuri Castle. Only four days had passed, but they had slept in dry beds and eaten warm food for the first time in months, and they were feeling alive again, even in the midst of so much death.

The fighting had moved well beyond Shuri, and it was safe here. Now that the Japanese had been driven from the caves underneath it and the castle itself had been destroyed, its red-and-gold pillars toppled and burned, Shuri Castle was nothing important anymore. Only one small part of a red wall still stood.

With all the trees gone, Shuri had an even more commanding view of the island, and for a time Hideki and Kimiko just sat and stared. To the south, the highways were clogged with dirty, injured, heartbroken refugees still caught in the cross fire. Gray smoke clouds and bright orange explosions all around them marked where the Americans and Japanese still fought. To the north, where once there had been a patchwork of lush pine forests and thatched farmhouses and green rice paddies, now there was nothing but muddy, barren hills with the nubs of shattered trees sticking up like the bristles on a spider.

Out at sea, American battleships still dotted the bay, little puffs of smoke and flame erupting from their big guns as they kicked the dead horse that was Okinawa. The skies finally clear, American planes buzzed over the whole island like flies over a corpse, strafing anything that wasn't already dead.

This was what their home looked like now. The battle would go on who knew how long, but once the Americans and Japanese were done with it, this was the Okinawa that Hideki and Kimiko would be left with.

Hideki took off the backpack he'd borrowed from American soldiers at the camp and unzipped it. From inside, he withdrew a picture of a young Japanese man and his mother—the photo one of the soldiers in the machine gun nest had given him while Kimiko and Masako and the others slipped past. Hideki had made a frame for the picture out of shards from a broken ammunition crate. Hideki walked over to the partial red wall of the castle that still stood. With a hammer and nails he'd borrowed from an American supply tent, he hung the framed picture up on the wall.

Hideki reached into the backpack for more photos and returned to the wall. He hung up the picture of a Japanese soldier and his girlfriend. And one of an American soldier and his children. And another of an American soldier and his dog. Hideki had made a frame for each of the photos out of rubble from the war, and now he hung each reverently, Americans alongside Japanese.

"So this is what you've been off doing all day while I've been working in the medical tent?" Kimiko asked.

Hideki didn't answer. Just kept hanging pictures. Dozens of them.

"Why are you honoring these soldiers who killed our people and wrecked our island?" Kimiko asked.

"I'm not," Hideki said. "Look. There aren't any soldiers here. There are brothers and fathers and sons, surrounded by the people they love and the people who love them back. I'm honoring the men they were before they came to Okinawa. Before they became monsters."

Kimiko looked at each of the pictures as Hideki hung it, then turned to stare at him.

"Why do you keep looking at me like that?" Hideki asked his sister.

"You've changed," Kimiko told him. "You're more confident. Braver."

Hideki snorted. "I'm not brave."

"Yes you are." Kimiko pointed down to the war raging on to the south. "You came all the way through *that* to find me."

"But I was scared the whole time."

His sister shook her head with exasperation. "Hideki, when are you going to learn that being brave doesn't mean not being scared? It means overcoming your fear to do what you have to do. A real coward would have run away and never looked back. Fear isn't a weakness. Anybody who's never been afraid is a fool."

Hideki felt the world spin underneath him. What his sister said actually made sense. He'd always been ashamed of his fear, but she was right—fear in the face of something truly terrifying, something you couldn't possibly hope to defeat, that wasn't weakness. It was natural. Logical even.

His ancestor Shigetomo, he wasn't a soldier. He was a farmer. So why had Hideki and his other descendants expected him to fight back against trained samurai warriors? There was never any chance he could have fought the Japanese and won. It would have been suicide.

Like me and my father being sent out to fight the Americans, Hideki realized. Neither of them had the right training, the right equipment.

Brave? I was so scared I pissed my pants. I was hit as I was running away. That's what his father had told him before he died. Hideki understood that fear. He'd felt it himself.

All that death and destruction around him—he'd had every right to be afraid. So why should he blame Shigetomo? Or himself? There were some horrors you couldn't fight and couldn't change. The real courage was just in enduring them.

Hideki felt an invisible weight lift off him, like when a *kijimunaa* finally got off his chest in the morning after a nightmare and he could breathe again. He felt a lightness, a release, as if he could float up into the sunlit clouds. Now that Shigetomo's cowardice had been forgiven and understood, his *mabui* was gone. Hideki was sure of it. Shigetomo's spirit was free to take its place in the afterlife with the rest of Hideki's ancestors, at peace at last.

But even as his heart soared with happiness and sympathy for Shigetomo, Hideki knew there was still something wrong with him. A sickness in his spirit that had nothing to do with Shigetomo or any of his other ancestors.

The last framed picture in the bag was Rei's. Rei and his father, laughing together. Hideki hung it in the center of the wall and his gaze lingered on it.

I'm sorry, Rei.

"Kimiko, there's something else," Hideki said. He didn't even want to say the words. Didn't want to admit the awful thing he'd done. But he had to. His sister was the only one who could help him. "Kimiko, I—I killed a man. An American soldier named Rei."

Kimiko didn't seem surprised. "I know," she said. "I can see his *mabui* on you."

"Can you free me from it?"

"Yes," Kimiko said. "I can help you find rest for his spirit. But that's not your biggest problem, Hideki. You've lost your own *mabui*."

"You mean Shigetomo's spirit?" Hideki said. "I know. I felt it go."

"Shigetomo is at peace now, yes," Kimiko said. "But that's not what I mean." She turned to look him in the eyes. "Hideki, *your mabui* is gone. The one you were born with. You lost it somewhere. It must have been knocked from you by something. Something violent and frightening."

Panic washed over Hideki, pulling him under like a wave. *The grenade.* The grenade he'd thrown at Rei had knocked Hideki's own *mabui* loose too! No wonder he'd felt so sick. So adrift. He'd lost his soul that day.

"How can I restore it?" Hideki asked.

"The only way is to go back to the place you lost it and find it and put it back."

"But—but I don't know exactly where I was when

I lost it." Hideki desperately scanned the hills all around them. Where had he been when he'd run into Rei? North of Shuri? South of Shuri? He couldn't remember.

Hideki watched the battles happening in the south and wondered about all the soldiers still fighting. Had they *all* lost their *mabuis*? Did all of them carry around an empty place inside them now too?

"Will I ever get my *mabui* back?" Hideki asked.

"Maybe. Maybe not," Kimiko told him. "You may go your whole life without ever getting your spirit back."

Hideki couldn't imagine feeling this hollow all the rest of his days. At least Hideki had Rei's *mabui* to borrow strength from. But that wasn't fair either.

Hideki looked at Rei's smiling face in the picture. Hideki couldn't deny Rei the peace he deserved just because he selfishly wanted to keep Rei's *mabui* for himself. He would do right by Rei first. Make sure his spirit found peace. Then Hideki would do what he could to restore his own spirit.

"That's him," Hideki said, pointing to the picture of Rei. Kimiko got up to look at it with him. "His name is Rei. He's the soldier I killed. I didn't want to," he said, tears falling down his face. "I only killed him because I was scared."

Kimiko hugged him, and Hideki let himself be hugged.

"You're still lucky, in a way," Kimiko said.

Hideki sniffed back his tears. "*Lucky?*" he said.

Kimiko nodded slowly. She was gazing out over the southern part of the island again, over the blasted hillsides and shattered trees. "You see only one ghost. But me, I see them all," she said. "The Americans. The Japanese. The Okinawans. All the spirits ripped so violently from this world. We'll spend the rest of our lives trying to bring them peace, and still we won't be able to heal them all. The sins of their *mabuis*, and the sins *against* their *mabuis*, they will leave a scar on this place for generations to come." Kimiko paused. "Their ghosts will haunt us forever. This is the end, Hideki."

Hideki made a rectangle with his fingers, framing a picture of Okinawa. But this time he didn't see the blasted, gray landscape of the present, or the simple green fields and red-and-white villages of the past. Instead he saw the future. Tall buildings touching the clouds. Buses and cars crowding the streets. Fishing boats and passenger ships trolling the aquamarine sea. The trees were back too, and the fields, green and purple and pink. Shuri Castle, rebuilt, stood bright red against the high blue sky. This was Okinawa, alive again, and stronger than ever before.

And there in the corner, framed perfectly in the foreground, was his sister, Kimiko.

It would take work, but together, he and Kimiko and all the others who'd survived would restore the spirit of Okinawa. They would mourn their dead, reconnect with their ancestors, and build a new future for themselves.

"No," Hideki said. "This isn't the end, Kimiko. It's a beginning."

AUTHOR'S NOTE

Throughout this book, American characters use the word "Jap"—short for Japanese—to refer to Japanese people. While the use of this term was common among soldiers and the American public during World War II, calling someone a "Jap" is offensive and disrespectful. I used this word in my book for historical accuracy, but it's a word you should never use.

In Japan, as in other places in Asia, people list their family name first, then their given name. Thus, Hideki Kaneshiro would actually be known as Kaneshiro Hideki. To avoid confusion among American readers, I reversed the order of Japanese names in this book to follow Western naming conventions.

The Battle of Okinawa began on April 1, 1945, and lasted 83 days, ending on June 22, 1945. It was the last battle of World War II, and the bloodiest of the Pacific War. The Americans brought nearly 1,500 ships and more than half a million men to invade an island defended by a combined Japanese and Okinawan force one-fifth that size. At the beginning of the battle, the population of Okinawa was just an estimated 450,000 people.

Just before the fighting began, the Japanese army encouraged civilians to relocate to northern parts of the island or to evacuate completely. But it was too little too late. The *Tsushima-Maru*, a Japanese transport ship, left Naha Harbor in August of 1944 filled with Okinawan refugees bound for mainland Japan. But because the Japanese used the same ships to deliver troops and weapons to Okinawa as they did to evacuate refugees, US submarines couldn't know if a Japanese ship was filled with soldiers or civilians. The *Tsushima-Maru* was sunk by the USS *Bowfin* shortly after the Japanese ship left port, killing 1,375 Okinawan refugees, including 777 children. Refugee transports were soon abandoned, leaving around 300,000 Okinawans still in harm's way.

The Imperial Japanese Army knew they were never going to hold on to Okinawa, and before the Americans arrived the most elite Japanese troops were withdrawn to prepare for what everyone assumed would be the eventual invasion of mainland Japan. To bolster their troops on Okinawa, the IJA conscripted 110,000 Okinawans into the army—about one-fourth of the island's entire population. Of that number, around 2,300 were students drafted from Okinawa's middle and high schools. Boys over the age of fourteen were first used to dig caves and build airfields. Then, as the conflict drew closer, they were drafted into the Blood and

Iron Student Corps or the signal corps of IJA infantry and artillery units. Girls were conscripted into student medical corps and put to work as nurses in IJA hospitals and command posts. Neither group was well trained or well organized, and almost half the young people forced to serve in the Japanese army died in the battle.

The Imperial Japanese Army fought a war of attrition on Okinawa, trying to wear down the US forces little by little as they advanced south. The US Tenth Army moved forward an average of 133 bloody yards a day for the first two months of the battle—little more than the length of a football field. GIs and Marines would fight for days to take a hill, only to find that at the last minute the Japanese army had abandoned the hill and withdrawn to fortify the next one. The US Army conquest of Kakazu Ridge—two small hills linked by a "saddle" in between them—took more than two weeks and cost the lives of hundreds of Americans and thousands of Japanese.

Throughout the battle, innocent Okinawan civilians suffered and died. Japanese soldiers often ejected them from the safety of tombs and caves or forced them at gunpoint to go out for food or water during bombings. The IJA used Okinawans as human shields, strapped explosives to Okinawans, and through propaganda and outright commands convinced Okinawans to commit mass suicide rather than be captured. While some

American soldiers tried to be conscientious about the differences between Okinawan civilians and Japanese soldiers, many more found it safer to throw grenades into caves or shoot machine guns through the wooden walls of houses, killing anyone inside, rather than risk their lives by investigating first. Thousands more Okinawans were killed by American battleships and planes as refugees fled south with the retreating Imperial Japanese Army in what has become known as the "Typhoon of Steel." Approximately one-fourth to one-third of the island's entire population died in the battle, including almost every Okinawan male over the age of eighteen.

The Imperial Japanese Army never surrendered, retreating all the way to the southern tip of the island and finally committing suicide when there was nowhere left to run. By the battle's end, 12,274 American soldiers and 110,000 Japanese soldiers were dead. The brutal fighting on Okinawa, and the Japanese commitment to fighting to the last man on what they saw as Japanese soil, made American soldiers and commanders alike believe that a full-scale invasion of mainland Japan would cost the lives of a million Americans and every last Japanese soldier and citizen. Though there is no direct proof, many military historians now believe that the lessons learned at the Battle of Okinawa were a direct factor in the United States' decision to drop atomic bombs on Hiroshima and Nagasaki two months later, which prompted Japan's unconditional surrender.

The United States occupied Okinawa after the war, finally returning control of it to Japan in 1972. But American military bases remain on Okinawa even today. An important part of America's strategic defenses in the Far East, Okinawa is home to thirty-two US military installations, which take up almost twenty percent of the island. The American presence is very controversial among Okinawans. In 2012, the United States agreed to reduce the number of US military personnel on the island, but the bases and ships and soldiers remain.

So too do thousands of bombs. According to Okinawa's Fire and Disaster Prevention Unit, several million shells and bombs were dropped on Okinawa by both sides during the battle, and an estimated five percent of them did not explode on impact. Many of them sank into the mud and muck, and remain there. From the end of the war until 1981, more than 6,000 tons of unexploded ordnance was discovered and disposed of, and more are found every year. Twenty hand grenades and 5-inch shells were found in a public park in Urasoe, and an inspection of a new site for a high school in Kadena uncovered one hundred rounds of armor-piercing antitank shells and nineteen hand grenades and naval shells. Officials estimate it may take another sixty or seventy years to clear Okinawa of all the remaining unexploded ordnance—if ever.

Many of the family tombs destroyed in the Battle of Okinawa were never rebuilt or were replaced by smaller burial chambers. But Okinawa as a whole has largely recovered and been restored in the decades since the end of World War II, becoming the bright, beautiful vision Hideki sees at the end. The capital city of Naha, which was completely destroyed by American bombs during the war, is a modern, shining metropolis of nearly 350,000 people. Kakazu Ridge is surrounded by apartment buildings. White Beach, where Ray and company landed on Love Day, is now one of the top-rated tourist beaches in the Pacific. Shuri Castle was rebuilt in 1992, and in 2000 was designated as a UNESCO World Heritage Site. Okinawa is a paradise once more, and its people are among the longest-lived on Earth.

At the southern tip of the island, at the site of the last fighting in the Battle of Okinawa and all of World War II, stands a monument called the Cornerstone of Peace. Dedicated on the fiftieth anniversary of the Battle of Okinawa, the Cornerstone of Peace lists the names of every single person who died during the Battle of Okinawa or because of it, Japanese and American and Okinawan, soldier and civilian alike. It is a memorial not to war but to peace, not to victors but to victims. Like Hideki's wall of photographs, it honors the men and women and children listed there not as soldiers or conscripts or refugees, but as the people they were before war swept them away. New names are added every year.

GLOSSARY

Artillery—large, long-range, land-based guns

Banzai—(Japanese) "Long life"; short for "Long Live the Emperor!"

Bashōfu—(Japanese) cloth made from banana fibers

Battleship—a heavy, armed warship with large, long-range guns

Bayonet—a blade attached to the end of a rifle for hand-to-hand fighting

Browning Automatic Rifle (BAR)—a heavy, rifle-like machine gun

Cover fire—gunfire meant to keep the enemy from shooting back

Cruiser—a fast warship with smaller guns and less armor than a battleship

Deferment—permission to put off military service until a later date

Destroyer—a warship that is smaller and faster than a cruiser

Dojin—(Japanese) "primitive animals" or "natives"; used as an insult

Emperor—the ruler of an empire; Hirohito was emperor of Japan during World War II

Entrenching tool—a collapsible shovel

Go (game)—a Chinese strategy board game played with black and white stones

Hajichi—(Japanese) indigo tattoos worn on the back of Okinawan women's hands

Haka—(Japanese) a turtle-shaped Okinawan family tomb built into a hillside

Imperial Japanese Army (IJA)—the official ground forces of the Empire of Japan during World War II

Kamikaze—a Japanese airplane loaded with explosives for a suicide run against enemy ships

Kanji—(Japanese) a system of Japanese writing using Chinese characters

Kanpan—(Japanese) hard, dry biscuits given as rations to Japanese soldiers

Kijimunaa—(Okinawan) small wood sprites from Okinawan mythology

Kimono—a long, loose robe with wide sleeves and tied with a sash

Lieutenant—a commissioned officer in the military; ranked above a sergeant

M-1 rifle—a semiautomatic rifle that was used during World War II

Mabui—(Okinawan) in Okinawan religion, the spirit, soul, or sense of self

Machine gun nest—A small, fortified position with room for a free-standing machine gun and its operators

Major—a military officer of high rank

Marines—the United States Marine Corps; a branch of the US Armed Forces

Mortar—a short gun for firing bombs at high angles

Prefecture—a district under the control of a government

Private—a soldier of the lowest rank

Sergeant—a noncommissioned officer in the military; ranked above a private

Sherman tank—a medium-sized tank used by the United States in World War II

Shisa—(Okinawan) a cross between a dog and a lion

Star shell—an ammunition shell that bursts in midair and produces a bright light to illuminate enemy positions

Sute-ishi—(Japanese) in the game of Go, stones played with the intention of sacrificing them

Yōkai—(Japanese) a ghost or phantom

Yuta—(Okinawan) in Okinawan religion, a person, usually a woman, believed to have the ability to talk to the dead

ACKNOWLEDGMENTS

Thank you to my amazing editor Aimee Friedman, and to publisher David Levithan, for their continuing faith and support. Huge thanks as well to the experts who read *Grenade* and helped me get my facts right, including Trent Reedy, Mitsuyo Sato, and Mieko Maeshiro. Any mistakes that remain are my own. Thank you to my copy editor Bonnie Cutler and my proofreader Susan Hom for making me look like I know what I'm doing.

And once again, I owe a huge debt of gratitude to everyone who works behind the scenes at Scholastic to make my books such a success: Ellie Berger, president of Trade Publishing; Tracy van Straaten and Crystal McCoy in Publicity; Mindy Stockfield, Rachel Feld, and Vaishali Nayak in Marketing; Lizette Serrano, Emily Heddleson, Michael Strouse, Matthew Poulter, and Danielle Yadao in Library and School Marketing and Conventions; Aimee's assistant, Olivia Valcarce; Melissa Schirmer, Cheryl Weisman, Leslie Garych, Catherine Sisco, Joanne Mojica, and everyone in Production; designer Nina Goffi for another fabulous cover and interior layout; map artist Jim McMahon; Jazan Higgins, Stephanie Peitz, Meghann Lucy, Jana Haussmann, Ann Marie Wong, Robin Hoffman, and everyone with the School Channels; Alan Smagler, Elizabeth Whiting,

Jackie Rubin, Alexis Lunsford, Nikki Mutch, Sue Flynn, Chris Satterlund, Charlie Young, and everyone in Sales; Lori Benton, John Pels, and Paul Gagne for their amazing work on the *Grenade* audiobook; and all the sales reps and Fairs and Clubs reps across the country who work so hard to tell the world about my books.

Special thanks to the writers at Bat Cave who heard me talk about this story for years, most especially to my friend and fellow writer Carrie Ryan for her eleventh hour critique that made a world of difference. Thanks as always to my friend Bob. And big thanks to my literary agent Holly Root at Root Literary, and to my publicists and right-hand women Lauren Harr and Caroline Christopoulos at Gold Leaf Literary Services—the work you do allows me to do the work *I* do. And thanks again to all the teachers, librarians, and booksellers out there who put my books into the hands of young readers—you're awesome! And last but never least, much love and thanks to my wife, Wendi, and my daughter, Jo.

Read more captivating novels from ALAN GRATZ!

Josef, Isabel, and Mahmoud come from different countries and different times in history, but they all have one mission in common: escape. All three kids go on harrowing journeys in search of refuge. All will face unimaginable dangers—from drownings to bombings to betrayals. But there is always the hope of *tomorrow*. This highly acclaimed *New York Times* bestseller tackles topics both timely and timeless: courage, survival, and the quest for home.

Ten concentration camps. Ten different places where you are starved, tortured, and worked mercilessly. It's something no one could imagine surviving. But it is what Yanek Gruener has to face. Can he make it through the terror without losing his hope, his will—and, most of all, his sense of who he really is inside? This astonishing tale of survival is based on the true story of Yanek (Jack) Gruener.

World War II is raging. Michael, originally from Ireland, now lives in Nazi Germany with his parents. Like the other boys in his school, Michael is a member of the Hitler Youth. But Michael has a secret. He and his parents are spies. When Michael learns about Projekt 1065, a secret Nazi plan to build a new kind of airplane, he may risk losing everything to steal the blueprints . . . including his own life.

Kamran Smith has it all. When he graduates from high school, he can't wait to join the Army like his older brother, Darius. But everything implodes when Darius is accused of being a terrorist. Kamran knows it's up to him to clear his brother's name. In a race against time, Kamran must piece together a series of clues that will lead him to Darius—and the truth. But is it a truth Kamran is ready to face?

ABOUT THE AUTHOR

Alan Gratz is the *New York Times* bestselling author of several books for young readers, including *Refugee*, a *New York Times* Notable Book and an Amazon, *Kirkus Reviews*, and *Publishers Weekly* Best Book of the Year; *Projekt 1065*, a *Kirkus Reviews* Best Book of 2016; *Prisoner B-3087*, a Junior Library Guild selection that was named to YALSA's 2014 Best Fiction for Young Adults list; and *Code of Honor*, a YALSA 2016 Quick Pick. Alan lives in North Carolina with his wife and daughter. Look for him online at alangratz.com.